Mafietta 3
Daddy's Little Girl

E. W. Brooks

DEDICATION

To all of my sisters who kissed a pond full of frogs before finding their prince.

1 DADDY'S LITTLE GIRL

The water spilled over Clarke's eyelids as her father held open both his hands and invited her into his arms for one last hug as his unmarried daughter. She closed her eyes and allowed herself to drift away into memories of happy times. Times when things were simple and his smile could change the course of her entire day.

Clarke missed talking to her Dad. She felt guilty for not calling him more, but he could hear her voice and instantly know what kind of day she was having. His discernment made conversations difficult these days. There was no way Clarke could ever allow her father to meet Mafietta. How could she explain her involvement in this crazy new family? Would he ever understand?

Clarke needed the shelter she found in his arms. She inhaled her last breath as Daddy's Little Girl and pushed herself off his chest as he looked down into her eyes and said, "Baby, I know this man makes you happy, but you don't have to do this."

Clarke hid her fear so far below her love for Errol that she hardly felt it as she responded, "But I love him, Daddy. He makes me happy."

"I hear ya, Baby Girl. Just know you always have a place in my heart and in my home. You always have a place to go. I know you won't need it. I just had to tell you." Clarke's father responded.

He kissed her on the check and brushed away the tear hanging from her eyelash. Liza-Beth Rushing was right on cue, as her knock ended their sentiments. This mighty father and his daughter shared a smile as Liza-Beth asked, "Clarke, are you ready? It's time."

Clarke fought the urge to break down and trust her father to get her away from the madness, but thought about everything that would hang in the balance. She, instead, squeezed her father's hand and they began to walk towards beautifully decorated double doors that opened into the sanctuary. Eric Benet's, "I Wanna be Loved" filled the room, as the soloist belted out lyrics that reminded Clarke why she fell in love with Errol in the first place.

Errol Bellow, King of the Port City, felt a gasp that echoed from his soul as he saw his wife-to-be for the first time in her pearl and crystal studded, wedding gown. He felt relief as he recognized the woman who made him live again. Emotions welled over and dripped from his face to his silk ascot, as he thought of all the sacrifices she'd made to be with him.

In this moment, on this day – his only desire was to please her. He promised her clean hands and from this point forward, she would have them. He was back to sit on the throne and now she could take her rightful place beside him. She was beautiful and she loved him – as ugly as he and this life could be – she loved him. That was enough for his forever.

The song and the aisle seemed too long. By the time Clarke and her father reached Errol, his attention was immediately transferred to his new father-in-law. He quickly slid his hand across his forehead and into his pocket. Errol was intrigued. Was Magnus making the sign to have a meeting?

Rev. Dubois' voice filled the sanctuary as he asked, "Who gives this woman to be wed?" Magnus ran his hand across his forehead and down to his pocket again before saying, "Her mother and I." Clarke noticed a quick look of perplexity on Errol's face, but it was quickly replaced with a smile, as Magnus gave him her hand and stepped away.

The nuptials were beautiful and there wasn't a dry eye in the building, as Rev. Dubois presented Mr. and Mrs. Errol Bellow to the world. A thunderous applause rose up from their friends and family when The Bellows sealed their marriage with a kiss.

Errol and Clarke were all smiles as they made their way out of the sanctuary and into the church vestibule, where Liza-Beth was waiting.

"Clarke, you have to head back to your dressing room

for makeup before the crowd leaves the sanctuary."

Errol smiled and shrugged his shoulders as his new bride was whisked away. He turned to find Rocko standing within inches of his face.

"What's up man?" Errol asked, surprised to find Rocko standing so close.

"Unc wants to see you, man." Rocko replied. "He's waiting in the pastor's study."

"Okay, thanks." Errol called as he headed down the corridor to meet his father-in-law.

Errol knocked on the door.

 "Come in."

Errol entered the office to find Magnus sitting at the pastor's desk. Rev. Dubois was standing to his right with his robe open and arms crossed.

"Wassup Magnus, you called for me?" Errol asked.

"Yeah I did, Youngblood. Have a seat."

Errol scanned the room and he could swear Rev. Dubois had a sliver nine peeking through his robe. He began to feel a wave of anxiety as Magnus leaned over the desk to face him.

"I know my baby girl loves you and I am coming to you as you should have come to me when you wanted to marry her." Magnus began.

"I don't understand, I did ask you for her hand." Errol replied as a look of utter confusion covered his face.

"Yeah, but you didn't tell me things were so hot and heavy for you." Magnus grimaced.

"Hot and heavy. I don't know what you mean." Errol responded, now obviously uncomfortable. "I think I'd better be going. Clarke is probably looking for me." He stood to rise and Rev. Dubois stepped into his path and pulled back his robe to expose a shiny gun.

"What the hell is going on here, Magnus? You got a strapped preacher steppin in my face. You better come correct, real quick man. You've obviously got me mixed up." Errol remarked defensively.

"Nah, Son. I have you exactly right. Now sit your ass down before my daughter hears of an accident that cost her husband his life." Magnus seethed.

Errol, not used to being railroaded, sat in his seat and looked at Magnus attentively.

"Well, now that I have your attention. I called you in here to let you know you have my support." Magnus began.

"Thank you. I am sure your daughter would appreciate that, but did you have to show me a gun to bring your point home?" Errol asked.

"No, fool." Magnus retorted. "This is not about my daughter. This meeting is about that reckless stunt you pulled today, blowing up cars and shit."

"I don't know what you're talking about." Errol replied attempting to remain cool.

Rev. Dubois was in his face before he could get out his next word.

"Don't lie to me, Errol. I wouldn't ask a question I didn't already know the answer to." Magnus said.

"Yo, Pops, tell the good pastor to get his gun outta my face." Errol hissed through clenched teeth.

Magnus nodded and Rev. Dubois lowered the gun.

"I'm not here to threaten you, Son. I kinda hoped you'd tell me the truth. I can't stand a liar. I usually shoot them." Magnus said as he and Rev. Dubois' laughter filled the room.

"Is this some kinda joke, Pops?" Errol asked, finally breathing a sigh of relief.

"Hell no, this ain't no joke. That stunt you pulled today is gonna cause some serious blow back. I am here to politely let you know that I got your back. You see, Rev. Dubois and I are hustlas from way back. We peeped your game early and there was no denying it, especially after you tried to bribe him with a church bus."

"Yeah, that was probably a bad move." Errol responded.

"Which move?" Magnus asked condescendingly.

"I probably shouldn't have had them blown up. That part was probably a bad idea."

"You damned right it was. That boy's brother has a hit out on your dumb ass right now. I bet you thought Mandell had your back, right? Nah baby boy, he's behind this shit. I think your throne makes him a little uncomfortable." Magnus advised.

"You can't say that. How do you know? You have no affiliation with the Kings." Errol growled. "Don't presume to know my business."

"Don't presume to know mine. Do you think anything comes into this city that I don't know about? You and the Kings have been on my radar for years, but you guys moved in silence, didn't sell to kids, and stayed away from schools. There was no need to rock your boat and besides, I've gotten used to those payments you've been sending to my guy at the port."

"Lester is your guy?" Errol asked, obviously taken aback by this new information.

"Yep, so let me keep this simple. My daughter is in danger and so is my unborn grandchild. I can't have this Errol. We gotta have a meeting as soon as you get back from the honeymoon." Magnus instructed.

"What honeymoon?" Errol asked. "We decided to postpone our honeymoon until after the baby comes. Clarke didn't want to make the trek to the Maldives with swollen feet."

"I get that, but you gotta get my baby outta here until I get to the bottom of this mess."

"She won't hear of it, Magnus. She has a shower and a charity event planned within the next week or so; you know your daughter."

"I did know my daughter until I started hearing this "Mafietta" shit all over town. Her mother and I didn't raise her to know this kind of life. Why do you think she had no idea about my extra curriculars?" Magnus asked.

"She doesn't know?" Errol asked.

"Boy, are you deaf? No way I bring her into this. It really pisses me off to have kept her away from the life for her entire life, only to have her marry you."

"I know I'm not that guy on Wall Street, but I love your daughter and I will do everything in my power to protect her. Nothing will happen to her as long as I'm here."

"I know you love her and I know she loves you. That's the only reason I haven't offed your ass already." Magnus chuckled.

"I know we have a reception to get to, but I am here to

make you a deal. I won't kill you for bringing my daughter in this bullshit, but you have one year to get out." Magnus smiled as he gave his new son-in-law an offer he couldn't refuse.

"You know the Kings won't allow that. She made them a small fortune while I was away. She knows too much." Errol replied. "I've managed to buy some time until after she has the baby, though."

"That's good, Son. That's good. I'll send you more bodies and see what else I can find out about your wedding day fireworks. Don't worry about anything. I got you. Consider the Williams and Bellow families in an official partnership." Magnus ordered.

"Sounds good, Pops. Thanks for looking out." Errol responded hesitantly. "Now if you gentlemen don't mind, I need to get back to my wife."

"Sure." Magnus said.

Errol stood and headed for the door. He turned one last time as he heard Magnus' voice, "Oh Errol, if you wanna stop breathing – touch or threaten my daughter again and I will have you duct taped, burned, and sent home to your mother for Christmas. Do you understand?" Magnus asked.

"Yeah, I got it, but I love her Pops. Things got hot for a minute, but we're good." Errol said as he quickly turned the door knob.

"You'd better be." Magnus ordered as Errol exited the room, closing the door behind him.

2 A MOMENT IN TIME

Errol rushed down the hall to put distance between him and his gangsta ass father-in-law. How could he have missed that? Errol's mind was running at warp speed when he bumped into Liza-Beth.

"Hey there. You're just the groom I was looking for. We are ready for your group pictures now."

"Ok, great." Errol replied

"Are you okay, Mr. Bellow?" Liza-Beth asked. "You seem a bit unnerved.

"Yes, just the happiest man on earth." Errol responded. "Now, which way do I head for these photos?"

"Just around the corner and through the back exit. We are gonna do some pictures around the lake."

Errol turned to see Clarke heading in the same direction. His wife was beautiful as she made her way to the door, with one bridesmaid holding her veil and another, her train. It was a miraculous sight. Marrying Clarke was the one thing he did right. He loved her so much and chose to focus on that for the time being, as he ran across the vestibule to greet the new Mrs. Errol Bellow, with an earth moving kiss.

"What was that for?" Clarke asked, looking up at her

smiling husband.

"I just married my best friend and she's having my baby. My life is finally complete."

"Awww, Babe. That is so sweet. I love you and I am so glad you chose me. Now let's go get these pictures taken so we can par-tay!" Clarke laughed. Errol kissed her on the forehead and wrapped his arms around his wife, as they headed outside.

The camera flashes had just died when Tina rushed to Clarke with her cell phone. It was New Hanover Hospital. Dee was in critical condition, but she'd survived.

The news moved from the phone receiver to Clarke's ears. The words swirled around in her head and made her dizzy. Errol rushed to Clarke just as she began to slide to the floor.

"Someone get a doctor!" Errol screamed as Clarke laid, limp in his arms.

Clarke's cousin Dawna, doctor and bridesmaid, rushed to her side and began to take her pulse. She raised Clarke's arm and the lifeless limb fell, hitting her in the face.

Errol was paralyzed in fear as Dawna announced, "She's okay. She just fainted."

Errol could hear the massive sigh of relief from the friends and family that surrounded the new couple.

"What just happened?" Clarke asked as her nostrils became filled with the odor of smelling salts. She slowly moved her head from side to side as small drops of water pelted her face. Clark opened her eyes and there she was, lying in Errol's arms as his tears fell.

Clarke reached up to touch her husband's face, "It's okay, Babe. I'm back."

Errol revealed a grin so wide, that it filled the room. He swept Clarke away and off to her dressing room in the church. Magnus followed.

Errol placed Clarke on the small love seat nestled in the corner of the room.

"What happened back there? He asked. "Who was that on the phone?"

"It was New Hanover. Dee is not dead. She's been burned almost to death and is fighting for her life right now. She's in intensive care." Clarke answered coldly.

"What about Hiram?" Errol queried.

"Nah, I think he's still dead." Clarke responded. "What now?" She continued.

"Now we have to go . . ." Errol began.

Clarke began to wave her finger back and forth in front of Errol's face. "Clean hands, remember? I don't want to know what's next, but here's what I do know." Clarke said as she stood to face her husband. "Whatever happens, you'd better, not, lay a hand on her."

"Don't lay a hand on her. You know she has to . . ."

"Uh uhn!" Clarke returned. "You don't get to pull me back into this."

Clarke looked up to see her father walk through the partially open door.

"Is my baby alright?" Magnus asked.

"Yes, she's fine. We still need to get her checked out, though. We gotta make sure the baby's okay." Errol answered.

"This little one is fine. He's fluttering around in there. I can feel him." Clarke smiled; rubbing her belly.

"What did you hear on that phone call that sent you into such a shock, Baby Girl?" Magnus asked his daughter.

"I got great news on the phone, Daddy. That was New Hanover. Dee is in critical condition. They aren't sure if she'll make it, but they are doing everything they can." Clarke reported.

"Oh, I see." Magnus responded, face full of concern.

"Let's get over to the hospital." Clarke ordered.

"Not today!" Errol commanded.

"I guess you heard that, Baby Girl." Magnus chuckled.

"Are you two teaming up on me?" Clarke asked.

"You bet we are! It isn't often that a man's only daughter gets married." Magnus returned.

"We have to go check on Dee. We can't just leave her there all alone. We owe her this." Clarke tried to explain.

"You owe her nothing." Magnus spewed.

Clarke was immediately confused by her father's response. He was not being the caring and compassionate man she'd always known right now.

"What do you mean, Dad?" Clarke asked, obviously confused by her father's reply.

"I mean, I am going to send Rev. Dubois to check on Dee so we can at least enjoy our father/daughter dance. I only get to do this once. We gotta do it right." Magnus said as he hugged his daughter tight.

Errol smiled as he witnessed the embrace. He could also see Magnus mouth to him, "I'll take care of this."

For the first time since he'd been out, Errol felt he could trust someone outside of the family. He was actually relieved that he wouldn't have to move on this.

Putting your hand back into a sticky situation can get you stuck and Errol wasn't having that. He'd seen too many good guys go down for not being thorough, and he refused to be "that guy."

Errol stepped over to the duo and said, "Excuse me, Sir. Could I get my wife back?"

Magnus and Clarke released their embrace and Magnus kissed his baby girl on the forehead.

"Ok, Errol. Here's my baby. You take good care of her."

"I got this, Pops. Now if you'll excuse us, we have a room full of hungry guests awaiting our arrival. Don't worry about Clarke. Dawna is gonna put on her doctor's hat and check her out again, once we make it to the vineyard." Errol said convincingly.

"Alright, Youngblood. I'll meet you guys there." Magnus said and then he was gone.

"What are we gonna do?" Clarke asked.

"Clean hands, remember? We are going to our wedding reception. Are you ready to party, Mrs. Bellow?"

"You bet your sweet ass I am." Clarke responded jokingly.

Errol kissed his bride as he held her stomach in his hands. He would hold his family together no matter what.

3 THE LIFESAVER

Clarke allowed Errol to keep her away from the hospital for the entire weekend. Each time she mentioned it, he would insist that they enjoy their time together before real life started again. He wanted the time to "get connected."

"Did we not just have the best wedding Port City has ever seen?" Clarke reminisced.

"Yes, we did." Errol responded proudly.

"Didn't I just pleasure you in ways you never thought possible?" Clarke asked seductively.

"Yes, you certainly did!" Errol answered playfully.

"Are you happy?" Clarke asked.

"Of course baby." Errol responded.

"Are you satisfied?" Clarke continued to probe.

Errol pulled Clarke closer, weaved his fingers in her hair and said, "Absolutely" before planting her with a passionate kiss.

Clarke delved into Errol's mouth and begin to suck on his tongue in that special way that made his body tingle. She landed a passionate kiss first on his mouth, his cheek, then his forehead, his other cheek, his chin, and finally his nose.

"That's what I thought." Clarke said, before mushing Errol in the face and heading toward the shower.

"I'll be back." she said. "I just need some air."

"I know you're worried about Dee." Errol finally voiced. "I just don't think today is the best day to go by the hospital."

"And why is that?" Clarke inquired as she turned around, moving closer to Errol.

"Take some time for yourself, Baby. You always worry about everyone else. Go to the spa. Get your hair and nails done. Don't stress yourself out with Dee. We've had a great weekend. Let's not jump into things so quickly, okay?" Errol said as his eyes pleaded with Clarke to listen.

Finally, Clarke relented.

"Fine, Errol. I won't go to the hospital until I think I can handle it. Is that fair?"

"That's all I'm asking, sweetheart. Stop being Mafietta and let Daddy love on you a little bit." Errol said teasingly.

Errol gave Clarke a quick slap on the butt as she turned on her heels to head upstairs. She was going to the spa, and then she was going to the hospital.

Errol watched Clarke jog up the steps. As soon as she was out of sight, he went into his office to make a call. Errol fell back into the huge leather chair and reached for the phone.

"Magnus, we have a problem."

"Wassup Youngblood?" Magnus returned.

"I can't seem to keep that headstrong daughter of yours from the hospital. I had to send Black to go sit with Dee, just so she would relax and give me some."

"Hold on, Youngblood." Magnus interrupted. "That is my daughter and if you ever speak to me about her in that way again - you won't have to worry about Hiram's brother. I'll kill you myself."

"I'm sorry, Dad." Errol responded jokingly.

"Don't worry about it, Son. I'll take care of it. One thing I learned in this business is that there's is no place for loose ends. They only trip you up."

"Thanks, Man. I owe you one." Errol responded.

"Nah nigga, you owe me two." Magnus returned and then he hung up.

Errol had to laugh. He knew at the end of the day, he had the best father-in-law in the world. He was still smiling and shaking his head, as he turned off the lights in his office and headed to join his wife in the shower.

Errol smiled as he saw Clarke's silhouette through the steamy shower door. She was starting to show even more now and he loved it.

Errol pulled the draw string on his shorts and they fell to the floor. He opened the door to find Clarke covered in suds. Errol felt the blood rush to his crotch. Clarke turned to find her husband with a full smile on his face.

"What's the smile for?" Clarke asked.

"Can't I be in love with my wife?" Errol responded jokingly.

"You most certainly may." Clarke said as she batted her eyelashes flirtatiously.

Errol stepped closer to his beautiful Mafietta. He began to kiss her slowly and deeply. Her body immediately responded to his touch. He pulled Clarke close and began to rub her stomach. The idea that his legacy was just inside aroused him even more. He lifted his hands and began to gently caress the new full firmness of her chest. She let out a soft moan as he gently kneaded her breasts. Errol's hands moved slowly and methodically to Clarke's nipples.

Errol traced Clarke's erect nipple with his finger. Clarke gasped and began to pant. She had never been this sensitive to his touch before. Errol began to gently rub her nipples between his thumb and forefinger. This feeling gave Clarke a new feeling that bordered pleasure and pain and she liked it.

Errol could hear Clarke's breathing change. Her breaths quickened and his dick began to throb. Clarke saw that Errol was ready for her and began to stroke his shaft as the suds ran down her body onto his. Her hands circled his head and his grip on her nipples tightened just a bit.

"OUUUUUUUUUUUUUUUUCCHH!" Clarke belted.

Errol

"Hey, what's wrong? What did I do?" He asked.

"Sorry to yell Babe, but my breasts are sensitive and my nipples are another story all together. They have a mind of their own right now. I liked what you were doing at first because it kinda hurt and it kinda felt good, but then it really became too painful to bear."

"Oh, I'm sorry, Babe." Errol returned. "Let me see if I can make you feel better."

Errol began to circle one of Clarke's nipples with his tongue, while he gently circled the other with his finger. Clarke's moans began to echo through the shower. He took his free hand and began to massage her clit. He slide her button between his pointer and middle finger, and began to rub her spot frantically.

Clarke began to scream as her clit pulsated; the heat that filled her box evaded and was replaced with a feeling that felt so good – she could only acknowledge it by screaming. He increased the tension on her button and she began to pant again, but louder as her King ushered her into an orgasm.

Errol allowed his hands to explore Clarke's depths even more. She was still massaging his Johnson and he was ready to explode. He frantically slipped a finger into Clarke's sweet spot. He let out a moan as his finger explored her softness. He began slowly, but then began to plunge his finger in and out of Clarke's hole. He felt her walls tighten and she felt his penis get even harder as they came together.

"Errol, why are you trying to stall me?" Clarke asked, after they had sex for a second time and she had finally gotten dressed.

"I just thought you may be tired and want a snack after all of that work." Errol smiled.

"Ha ha. Nice try Mr. Bellow, but I'm getting outta that door." She gave her husband a quick peck on the cheek, and was on her way down the steps.

Errol rushed to his cell phone to call Magnus.

"What's up, Youngblood?" Errol's father in law asked.

"I held Clarke as long as I could, but you know your daughter. I couldn't stop her." Errol replied.

"I just got the whoop whoop for the wamp wamp, so it'll take me about 30 minutes to get there." Magnus explained.

"Clarke is going to the spa for a couple hours first, so you'll still be in good time."

"Alright, Son. Let me be about mine. I'll holla back later."

"Thanks Pops." Errol said awkwardly.

"No problem, Son. No problem at all." Magnus responded before hanging up.

Errol poured himself a drink, lit a spliff, and his next call was to Black.

"What's up mi Boss?" Black asked as he answered the phone.

29

"I need you to tail Clarke today." Errol ordered.

"C'mon, Man. No offense, but that woman has been evil lately. Can I pass on dealing with your pregnant wife?" Black asked jokingly.

"If anyone else said that, I'd shoot'em." Errol laughed. She is on her way to the spa downtown on Front Street then she's heading to the hospital to check on Dee."

"I gotcha," Black said. "I was coming from Smithfield's Barbeque on 17th Street when some dumb ass was on the phone and rammed the car in front of him. It caused a 4 car pile-up. So, I'm just sitting here right now." Black replied.

"No worries. Just get to her as soon as you can. I have a feeling she may need you. She's . . ."

Black couldn't let Errol finish his sentence. "Yo Errol, Clarke just drove by me, headed toward the hospital."

"Oh shit, Man. I gotta call Magnus. Let me hit you right back."

"Errol, what's going on man?" Black asked.

"I don't have time to explain. Just get turned around and keep Clarke with you, until I call."

Black heard a click and Errol was gone. He knew something must be up so he pulled his car up onto the median, and made a break in the other direction. Black was two blocks away from the hospital when he saw blue lights in his rear view mirror.

"Damn." Black screamed, as he pummeled the steering wheel with his fists.

Magnus was dressed in a black hooded shirt with a fitted cap pulled down over his eyes. He was wearing a pair of dark shades and a fake white moustache. He was barely recognizable especially since he wasn't wearing his thick gold link bracelet, or his diamond pinky ring. The one place Magnus couldn't take shorts was his feet. He was wearing his prized $60,000 autographed Nike Air Jordan 1 Sneakers.

He politely nodded at the young mother standing in the elevator next to him. He pressed number 4 and she, number 5. Magnus got out on his floor and gave each of the woman's five kids a $20 bill. He stepped off the elevator, turned left, and followed the descending room numbers until he reached room number 427. There was no one in the room with Dee. Her face was wrapped up and she appeared to be asleep.

The poor soul looked like a mummy and she was there all alone. Magnus reconciled that he would be doing Dee a favor by helping her to transition. He placed the small needle into the first port on the IV line. Dee's eyes opened momentarily. The permanent grimace on her face turned to a smile and within the next minute, she was asleep forever. Magnus said a prayer for them both, and quietly exited the room un-noticed.

He was rounding the corner to the elevator when he bumped into his daughter. She dropped her purse and Magnus immediately followed his instincts and knelt down to pick up the purse. Clarke looked downward toward the floor. She noticed the expensive sneakers this kind stranger was wearing.

"Nice shoes." Clarke remarked. "My dad has a pair just like them; with the autograph and everything."

The kind gentleman remained silent, but handed Clarke her purse. Clarke noticed the scar her father earned on one of their fishing trips long ago.

"Dad?" Clarke asked confused as she grabbed the man's scarred hand.

"Get down, Baby." Magnus yelled as he saw a man dressed in black round the corner, holding a glock with a silencer. The shooter fired three times as Magnus pushed Clarke to the floor and pulled a baby 380 from his shoe.

One shot pierced the shooter's head and the other, his heart. He fell dead immediately. Magnus called out to his daughter. She didn't respond and he called out again. This time his worst fears were realized. Clarke had been shot; once in the head and once in the stomach.

"HELP, HELP, HELP!" Magnus screamed as he lifted his daughter's body from the floor and ran toward the approaching doctors. They rushed Clarke to an operating room.

Errol Magnus Bellow was born a preemie at 3:57 pm, on September 17th. Clarke was in a coma.

4 A VISION OF LOVE

RUFUS HENRY

Clarke could hear a baby cry. She heard a voice that sounded like her father talking to Errol, but she wasn't sure. Her head felt so hazy. Clarke tried to open her eyes, but they weighed a ton. She mimicked the scene from Kill Bill and tried to will her hands and toes to wiggle.

She heard her husband say, "Dad, look. She just moved her fingers. Call the nurse." Clarke tried to stay awake, but she was just too tired. She couldn't hold onto her consciousness any longer. For Clarke, her visions seemed to last for months, but her soul needed this time to recalibrate and kick start itself again. Her body was shutting down to re-declare its intentions in this world.

As fate would have it, Clarke would have to take a walk down memory lane to get to the other side of this journey.

When Clarke came to, the room was hazy.

"What am I doing here?" Clarke asked herself as she sat across the table from Rufus.

Clarke couldn't understand why she was reliving this nightmare from her past. She was even more startled when the conversation in her dreams mirrored the one she'd had a few years back.

"I don't know what you tellin' me for. It ain't mine." Rufus sputtered.

Clarke almost spit out her coffee.

"What? You've been stuck in my face for the last year and a half, and now you can sit in front of me and say this isn't your baby? Are you serious?"

"Don't give me that shit, Clarke. You can't make me believe I was the only one you were messing with." Rufus responded.

"I am 3 and a half weeks pregnant. Do you know where that puts us?" Clarke asked.

"I don't know where it puts you. I ain't got nothing to do with this.'" Rufus returned.

"I'll tell you where that puts us. It puts you with me, smack in the middle of that one week trip to Arkansas when we visited your mother last month."

"Can't be mine." Rufus said before crossing his arms and staring back at Clark with dark unfamiliar eyes.

"Do you know who you are? One phone call will ruin you. That's something you should consider when you make reckless statements like that." Clarke hissed. "Now, I am going to work and when the waitress comes with the check, ask her if she can add a fucking clue to your tab, Asshole."

With that, Clarke was out of the door. She could hear her grandmother's words echo through her ear, "I don't care if you have to cry your pillow wet at night. You never let a man see you cry." Those words held her tears back like a dam, until she was out of the parking lot.

Clarke made the short drive back to her apartment. She began to feel hot and nauseous. She rushed up the stairs and barely made it to the bathroom before she was blowing chunks of IHOP pancakes into the toilet.

2 months later

"Hey, Cuz. How you feelin?" Macy asked. Clarke could feel the concern in her voice all the way from her barracks room in Iraq.

"I'm good, girl." Clarke responded trying to sound happy.

"Clarke, you know I already know better than that, right?" Macy asked mockingly. "I had a dream last night.

I know something's wrong. What is it?" She pried.

Clarke knew her cousin was thousands of miles away, but she needed a non-judgmental ear to help her through this. She immediately began to cry.

"Girl, if you don't stop crying." Macy barked. "You are having a child and there is nothing sad about that. You give that adulterer too much control over your life. Even if he never realizes the gift you are carrying; its okay, Clarke. You have the family and you know you got me." Macy said reassuringly.

"I know, Mace. It's just that I never expected to be here at 24. Don't you remember my plan: married by 24, two kids by 30, and retired by 45?" Clarke asked her sister.

"If life went the way we planned it all the time, there'd be no room for Jesus." Macy responded.

"Yeah, you're right. It's just that I thought I was exempt from shit like this. Bait and switch is something they do on Black Friday when everyone is shopping. It isn't something the lying ass man next to me should be doing to hide his wife from his mistress." Clarke responded.

"Girl, that's your problem! I don't know where you get this sense of entitlement, but just in case you didn't get the newsflash, let me bring it home for you. You are not exempt from life's bullshit. I know you think you're super special and all; you are, but you gotta lay in the bed you made, just like the rest of us." Her confidant advised.

"I had that dream again." Clarke said flatly.

"What dream?" Macy asked trying not to remember the details from a dream she'd heard twice already.

"You know what dream." Clarke returned. "I think Rufus is going to try to kill my baby."

"Girl, that clown may pretend to be shell shocked to get that government check, but he is far from being that stupid." Macy countered.

"If this gets out; he could lose everything. I watch Law and Order all the time, and that sounds like motive to me." Clarke joked.

"Then stay away from him, Clarke. If you have to talk to a snake, let him hiss in your ear while he's still under the rock, but never get close enough to let it bite you."

Clarke loved her cousin Macy. Things were always so black and white with her.

3 months later

Clarke was only 20 weeks pregnant and something was wrong. After a trip to the hospital and 3 hours of contractions, her baby was here, but he was dead. Rufus didn't make it to the funeral and he even refused to pay his half of the doctor and funeral bills.

Clarke cried out in her sleep as she felt the pain all over again. For a second, it was almost as if she could hear Errol telling her everything would be fine. She felt his hands rub hers. For now, all she could do was wiggle her fingers, but it was enough to let Errol know she was still there.

After a few minutes, Clarke's efforts had worn her down. Again she was immersed in an old and familiar, but uncomfortable setting. This time Clarke saw herself lying in her bed after her stillborn; depressed and alone.

Clarke's family was worried about her. She was home alone in her apartment and she wasn't answering her phone. They were afraid that Clarke was taking pills to sleep through her pain.

Clarke wasn't doing any of that. She was thinking. Her father insisted she needed some help and she'd begun to see Brenda, a therapist, to help her deal with the grief. Brenda suggested that Clarke continue to allow herself to feel the pain of losing her son, but then to reflect on any of the positive things that could be drawn from the situation. She even encouraged her to get back out there and date.

LAVON HILL

Lavon Hill came into Clarke's life just in time and for a season's reason.

"This fried chicken is banging. Do you know how long it's been since I've had home cooking?" Lavon asked as he reached for another drumstick.

"Don't they feed you Marines the best food there is?" Clarke teased.

"The D-Fac has banging breakfasts, for sure, and some of their stuff is good, but there's nothing like home cooking."

"Is it safe to say you like my chicken, or is it my mac and cheese?" Clarke asked jokingly.

"Hmmmmm, I'm not sure. Do you mind if I decide over a bottle of wine?" Lavon asked.

"Not at all." Clarke smiled. It felt good to flirt. She hadn't been in the company of a man for months.

"White or red?" Clarke asked.

Lavon handed Clarke a pink wine bag with a cute silver bow stuck to the top of a bottle of red wine from the local winery.

"So, I see you do have some manners." Clarke remarked.

"You're gonna love me." Lavon replied.

"Slow down, Soldier. Can we start with the cork screw for that wine?"

"I'm not a Soldier, I am a Marine." Lavon responded curtly.

"Well, excuse me Mr. Marine." Clarke returned awkwardly.

"It's Mr. Staff Sergeant Marine, to you." Lavon responded playfully.

"Whatever, Lavon." Clarke returned. "Can I call you that?"

"You can call me whatever you like, Baby."

Two glasses of wine later, Lavon was feeling a little buzzed. He drank with Clarke to set the mood for good unfiltered conversation, but he never expected the wine to faze him. He stood to leave, and began to feel a bit shaky. Clarke noticed his unsteadiness.

"Uhhh, I see you're a lightweight." Clarke joked. "You are welcomed to crash here, but don't think you're getting any."

Lavon pulled Clarke close to him. "Don't worry. I won't push you, but I promise you'll try to give it to me before I ask again."

"Whatever, man. I'm a country girl. We aren't built like that." Clarke smiled.

"We'll see." Lavon smirked. "But for now, is there somewhere I can lay down?"

"Sure." Clarke responded. "You can go get in my bed."

"You're gonna have to sleep with me." Lavon said, matter of factly.

"No, I'm not, dude. Did you really think it was gonna be that easy? You got me messed up." Clarke said, obviously offended.

"Nah, Clarke, it's not that. I've been to war, and you are nice and everything, but this is still a strange place for me. It will just make me feel better about being here. I'll hold you, but I won't try to push up on you. Is that fair?"

"Oh, Lavon." Clarke said as she kissed him on the forehead. "It would be my honor as an American citizen to sleep with you."

They both laughed. Lavon helped Clarke tidy up the kitchen and load the dishwasher before she showed him to the bedroom. Clarke tried hard not to seem too anxious, or show just how happy she was to finally have some male companionship.

"Hey. I gotta jump in the shower, but you can see the bathroom from the bed and I'll be right out."

"That's cool." Lavon said as Clarke turned back the covers for him.

Lavon took off his shirt and his chiseled chest immediately reignited a spark Clarke hadn't felt since before she had her baby.

"Dear Sweet Baby Jesus, let me get outta here." Clarke said as she fanned herself and headed toward the door.

"What's wrong?" Lavon asked.

"Oh, nothing. It's just getting a little hot in here. If you don't need anything else; I'm gonna jump in the shower."

"Nah, I'm good." Lavon responded as he pulled off his pants and stood there in his boxers. "I'm gonna go ahead and try to get some shut eye."

"Cool. I'll be right back." Clarke said as she grabbed a towel and bath cloth from the linen closet.

Suddenly, Clarke could hear Lavon laughing. Oh Hell, Clarke thought. This cat really is shell shocked.

"Hey Clarke, come here for a second." Lavon said through broken laughter.

Clarke walked back to her room to find Lavon sitting in her bed, swinging her vibrating bullet back and forth as he said, "Excuse me, Miss. Is this yours?"

Clarke wanted to die, but she smiled and responded, "Yes it is. I'll take that. Thank you." She walked over to Lavon and snatched the cord he had swinging from his fingers, as she joined him in laughter.

1 month later

Clarke and Lavon were inseparable. He made the hour and fifteen minute drive every night after work to be with her. She prepared dinner each evening, and they ate meals like any normal couple would. Their dynamic made her heart flutter. This is the kind of relationship Clarke always wanted.

Clarke's family finally stopped worrying about her. They were glad Lavon was there to help her enjoy life again.

Clarke and Lavon loved their routine. Clarke felt married. Her relationship with Lavon mirrored the one she would want to have with her own husband someday. She began to hope she and Lavon had a permanent future together. Clarke even made him a house key. They had something real. She just didn't know it was temporary.

2 months later

Duty called and Lavon was off to training in Twenty Nine Palms, California. He was becoming a recruiter. Clarke cried buckets the day Lavon left. Something within told her things would never be the same. Clarke prayed, wished, and willed Lavon back to his duty station at Camp Lejeune, but fate had other plans.

Lavon enjoyed the use of the cell phone in Clarke's name, but things were getting kinda flaky between the two of them, so Clarke decided to do a little digging. Clarke, the investigator, forwarded the calls from Lavon's cell to hers. Then she waited.

Sure enough, the phone began to ring, and finally the call came from the number that appeared on Lavon's phone bill almost as much as her own.

"Hello." Clarke answered.

"I'm sorry. I have the wrong number." The polite voice responded.

"It's okay."

A second call came to the phone.

"Hello."

"Wow. I'm sorry. I'm trying to call my fiancé and I think the lines are crossed or something, because I've gotten you twice." The happy voice responded, obviously proud of her man.

"Your fiancé'?" Clarke spewed. Are you talking about Lavon?" Clarke asked, sure that this wasn't happening.

"Yes, why?"

"He told me you were his cousin." Clarke returned in shock.

For the next 20 minutes, Clarke recounted the best two months of her life and politely answered questions. Thirty minutes later, Lavon called, cursed Clarke out, and told her never to call him again. She decided Lavon and the dummy deserved each other. There were still two weeks left before Lavon was due back from Twenty Nine Palms, and Clarke still had his Jeep. There was no way Clarke was meeting this clown after disrupting his beautiful lie.

Clarke decided to get even. Her tears turned to venom as she considered ways to make Lavon pay. That's when the idea came. Clarke drove about twenty miles out of her way to have dinner at Wrightsville Beach's Blue Water Grill. She must have gone through at least 10 stop lights and she ran them all. After a great steak and a mixed drink, Clarke took an even longer route home and slid through a few stoplights then, too.

Clarke made the same journey three more times before Lavon came to pick up his Jeep. His training was over and he was moving from North Carolina to Mississippi. Clarke's dreams of babies and a happy life with Lavon were over. She felt numb as she handed Lavon the keys to his truck.

"Clarke, you were good to me and you don't deserve this. I'm sorry." Lavon offered holding onto the keys and Clarke's hand.

Clarke stood there motionless. She refused to respond, but she nodded her head and jerked back her hand.

"I know this sounds crazy, but I love you. I wanted to be with you, but you said you'd never leave North Carolina. I'm a Marine, Clarke. I move for a living. How would something serious work with us? I have eight children, Clarke. Destiny knows me. She knows my bullshit and she was there for me when no one else was and I just can't let her down. I didn't expect to fall for you, Clarke. I thought I would just come through and get some ass. I never expected you to say, 'No.' on the first night. I never expected us to stay up talking for hours and I never, never expected to love you. You are the Yin to my Yang. We have chemistry. You don't let me get away with shit like she does. I need a strong woman like you. In a perfect world; you and I would be together, but

Destiny isn't strong like you. I've hurt her before and I just can't do it again. I have to marry her, but I will still love you. We can make this work, Clarke. I don't know how yet, but can we figure this out. Please. I can't give you up. You mean too much."

For the first time in the conversation, Lavon was able to finally get a bit of a reaction from Clarke. He saw a brief fire flicker through her eyes. Clarke thought back to more pearls of wisdom from her Grandmother, "I don't care how bad he's hurt you; you don't get into a cursing match. Sometimes a man doesn't deserve the comfort of your words. Stay silent, move on, and you'll never have to say I'm sorry."

Clarke extended her arms to the man she'd grown to love. She ignored her racing heart, sweaty palms, and the tightness in her chest. Clarke hugged Lavon.

Tears fell from his face. He'd never felt a love so pure and it killed him to see what he was doing to her. Clarke whispered in his ear. "You're gonna pay for this."

Lavon pushed her away. He needed to see her face. He was getting uncomfortable. Clarke was too calm. If she were cursing or trying to fight him, he would know how to handle her, but he didn't know what to do with quiet resolve.

He didn't see anger or vengeance in Clarke's eyes. He looked into her soul for the last time he'd ever have access, and he saw her pain, but he also saw her strength.

Clarke felt Lavon trying to read her, so she quickly shut her eyes to close the window.

"Congratulations and best wishes, Dude. I gotta go." Clarke responded. She walked away and never looked back.

1 month after the breakup

Clarke had a trying day at the office. She'd been so busy, she hadn't had time to respond the constant buzzing coming from her cell phone. There were 10 calls from the same unfamiliar number. Clarke started her car and headed home when her quiet drive was interrupted by another call.

"Hello." Clarke answered.

"I just got $3000 in stop light tickets, Bitch. How many stoplights did you run? Who gone pay this shit? I'm not paying it. That's real fucked up, Clarke."

"Ditto." Clarke responded. She hung up on Lavon, and then she laughed through her tears for the rest of her drive home.

Clarke's blood pressure rose as she found herself sitting in the back of her best friend's Jeep. Clarke remembered this scene very well. It was the final pit she'd fallen into before getting herself together. This was the wound that hurt the most, because this failure sat solely and squarely on Clarke's shoulders. It was all her fault and she refused to go to her father to bail her out again. Clarke tried to think of something else, but this vision was different than the others. She couldn't stop it.

Clarke didn't panic though. She could feel the universe opening up to give her inspiration for the next leg of her journey. Her visions had taken her through the dark hole of her soul, but Clarke didn't feel condemned by it. Her third eye began to explain what she'd been through and why.

Clarke tried to open her eyes, but instantly she yielded to the latest vision playing itself on the inside of her eyelids. Her spirit began its documentary. Clarke's voice narrated.

It wasn't when I kissed my baby and gave him back to God that inspired me. It wasn't when he threw a glass of wine in my face or refused to pay for half of the doctor bills or the baby's funeral, that the light came on.

It wasn't – when, I moved out of that leaky cold $750 apartment into a place with lower rent in a nicer neighborhood; when I lost it all, got evicted, was forced to turn my back on that bridge and everyone on the other side of it that I became inspired, either.

I had nothing but the clothes on my back, the ones in the hamper, some papers I'd managed to save by stuffing them into a fake Louis Vuitton purse with worn handles, and two pairs of shoes.

As my best friend drove me across the Holmes Bridge to my new life in the unknown, I had time to reflect. I could see every bad decision I'd made and how they led me here.

I wished I could go back and pay the rent I wore to the party. I wish I wouldn't have pretended to be able to afford all of those drinks at the bar or the outfit for my home girl. I'd blown about eighteen hundred dollars and managed to miss every bill. Nothing was paid. That was the mistake.

I woke up to the sheriff and the handyman knocking at my door. They'd come to change the locks. It was over. My life had officially fallen apart.

Were these the kind of seeds I'd sown? The rough tough, but honest answer was YES. I did this.

I'd known hurt all my life. I grew used to ridicule and didn't know how to accept a compliment. I was a mess.

I couldn't explain my reason for being. I was lost and this was the consequence.

We met my cousin in a town about an hour away. I stood there and fought back tears, as we moved everything I owned from one trunk to the other. I was at rock bottom. I was ashamed and embarrassed. I was homeless, my car had been repossessed and I was sleeping on my cousin's couch.

I couldn't take a bottle of sleeping pills or slit my wrists. I refused to let these lessons be for naught. I was here. I would be better. I would be the woman God created me to be. I had nothing. I had to start from here and I would. I had nothing, but finally, something was different.

I felt love. It wasn't a familiar feeling. I didn't even understand it at first. It was a love for something new – uncharted and unfamiliar. It was a love for self. I realized for the first time, why I suffered.

I'd never known how to love myself. I never felt worthy of the love of others and always tried to buy it, and I didn't even have the sense to make sure I had shelter in the process. I had been a fool. I was finally willing to accept it. I wasn't lying anymore. I was happy. I was inspired by my pain. I had learned Karma's lesson and it was time to move on.

That was two years ago.

Now I can accept it when someone tells me how nice I look or how big my heart is without crying. The day I lost everything was the day I gained it all!!

That is the day I found my laugh. That was the day I gained real life perspective.

Clarke had worked so hard to bury that moment of failure. Reliving that time opened the vault to her deepest fear. That was to end up alone and with nothing. She and Errol could always start over, but she just couldn't be without him. That would kill her.

Despite Clarke's crazy life, she was happy. Clarke hadn't seen her son yet, but she knew, without a shadow of a doubt that he was alive and well. Her life with Errol wasn't perfect, but it was theirs; it worked for them.

Errol didn't use her, like Rufus. He didn't lie to her, like Lavon. He'd never tried to hurt her and she knew he would always put their family first, despite his role as the head of the Port City Kings. Clarke began to see moments from her wedding play back in her head. She felt Errol's hand on her leg. It touched her to have him there. She wasn't sure how long she'd been out, but she was definitely ready to wake up now. Her life was amazing and she was ready to get back to it.

She filled her body with gratitude. Clarke was blessed and she knew it. She began to laugh, first in her spirit and then it must have filled the room because Errol rushed to Clarke's side and began to squeeze her hand.

"Come on, Baby. Come back to me. Come back to your family. We love you. Please, don't leave us. We need you. Come back to me, Baby and I promise to make you laugh every day, just as you're laughing now."

Clarke felt the weight of the world being lifted. Suddenly, she knew she had to come back to her world. There was no need to be ashamed of her past. It made her who she was. She wasn't wrong for giving those assholes her heart. They were wrong for abusing it. Clarke always tried to make her relationships work and that's where she'd gone wrong.

Relationships are work, but they are much easier when both people pull their weight. So what, if she was married to a drug dealing assassin; the same God that protected her up until now would continue to look out.

All of those other guys were preparation for her life with Errol. The pain she felt when she buried her son was a lesson in treasuring the things that matter. Losing a son, so long ago, made Clarke appreciate the chance to get to know this new extension of her even more. She wondered what Errol named him. They never discussed it.

Oh, Lord. She thought. *What did this man name my*

baby? You know he's not from the US. Lord, please send me back. I need to be with my son.

Clarke's spirit had been filled with a charge. She was going back home, but she had some major changes to make. It was her job to save herself and her family. Clarke began to visualize a happy and healthy family. She saw Errol laughing that deep and hearty laugh as he played with his son. She saw a family complete and at peace. This picture was the last thing Clarke saw before she opened her eyes.

"Errol, where is my baby?" Clarke asked.

Errol was asleep in a cot on her right. A small bassinet separated them. She could see her son. He was alive and healthy. Her Dad was on the other side, to her left, on a pleather couch with his long legs hanging over the side. Errol's brother, Admiral, was in the hospital bed on the other side of the room and Black was standing beside the door.

He was the first to see Clarke.

"Errol, Errol – wake up, Man." Black said loudly.

"What? What is it?" Errol asked rubbing his eyes as Clarke's father began to stir on the couch.

Clarke began to cough. Errol jumped to his feet.

Admiral went to get a nurse.

"I wanna see my baby" were Clarke's next words.

Errol picked up his namesake proudly. Then he lowered his son to Clarke's chest. The baby instantly recognized the smell of his mother and clung to her chest as he slept. Clarke kissed her son and thanked God for his safe arrival.

Errol leaned over and kissed his wife.

"I am so glad you came back to me."

"How bad is it?" Clarke asked.

"Baby, you're just waking up. You don't have to get all Mafietta right now." Errol responded.

"How bad is it?" Clarke asked raising her voice.

"They tried to kill you, Clarke." Errol reported sadly. "I know what I promised. I know I promised you're a life with no more blood on your hands, but I have to protect my family. You have to understand what has just happened. I could have lost you and our son."

'Kill them all." Clarke whispered.

Errol, obviously shocked by Clarke's demand, said, "What? You don't mean that. We'll be at war."

Suddenly, Clarke didn't feel the scratchiness or soreness of her throat.

"You don't' know what my life was like before you

came. You have shown me what it's like to have my love be reciprocated. Errol Bellow, you taught me how to love. You have given me a home and a family of my own and it's all worth fighting for." Clarke said stroking her son's hair.

"My family is all I have. I won't tolerate this. It's time they meet Mafietta 3.0."

5 HUSTLIN IS IN MY BLOOD

Watching Errol switch back and forth between Super Dad and the Kingpin Overlord a site to see. The entire team was in love with little Errol Magnus Bellow and if they're loyalty to The Kings wasn't enough; there was no way they were letting any harm come anywhere near that baby.

Errol and his father-in-law worked together like a well-oiled machine. This made Clarke happy. She sat in the corner and laughed to herself as the two competed for the little one's attention. Errol held his son close as Magnus sat nearby enjoying the view.

For the first time since her return from the hospital, she was ready to talk about what happened. Clarke's face and countenance changed. Black was the first to sense it. Clarke nodded to her old friend and he took their bundle of joy upstairs to Anna for his afternoon nap.

Admiral looked to his brother, waiting to see if it was okay to bring everyone up to speed. Errol shook his head no and stood to leave the room as Clark interrupted him.

"No, Sir. You can just have a seat."

Mangus stood up to leave and Clarke stopped him dead in his tracks too.

"You too Daddy."

Magnus let out a sigh, knowing he could no longer hide the truth from this baby and he fell into the butter soft leather of the oversized lounge chair dreading the impending conversation.

"Well, hubby? When did you and Dr. Kevorkian decide to kill my friend?" Clarke asked.

"You knew we couldn't leave her out there with all of the information she had. You said yourself that she wanted to ruin you." Errol responded.

"Honey, that baby was burnt up like old fish grease. She was in pain, Clarke. This may not be the answer you want to hear, but we helped that girl by putting her out of her misery. She saw me before I stuck the needle in her IV and she smiled. She was ready to go, Baby." Magnus explained.

"How could you two do this and not tell me first. You didn't let me say good bye. She was good to me. I am the one who wronged her. I owed her." Clarke said getting choked up. I owed her, at least, a goodbye and an apology and you two took that away from me."

"You wanted clean hands, Babe. I just wanted to see that you had them." Errol advised.

"Enough with this clean hands, shit. This mother fucker could have killed me and my baby. I want his head and I want it now." Clarke yelled.

"Do you know what you are asking?" Admiral asked.

"Yeah, I know what I'm saying. That dread head bastard came after me and mine and now I want blood from everyone he knows."

"Calm down, Baby." Magnus chuckled. It tickled him to see his daughter throw this tantrum.

"Don't tell me to calm down, Daddy. I'm the one with the bullet holes."

"You're running around the city calling yourself Mafietta. Did you not think you'd ever have to take a bullet?" Magnus asked his daughter.

Errol chuckled.

An infuriated glance from Clarke quickly ended her husband's laughter.

"Baby girl, you can get mad all you want to, but you just earned the title you carry. The streets love you. They've made you a legend. They seem to have forgotten that I open the doorway to three quarters of the East Coast. Nah, that doesn't matter. It's all about Mafietta now. You stole my shine, baby." Magnus said shaking his head.

"Ummmm, about that. Dad, why didn't you ever tell me what you really did for a living?" Clarke asked, refusing to contain the burning question any longer.

The room fell quiet.

"Admiral, let's go check on Junior. These two need some privacy." Errol suggested.

Magnus searched for words as the doors quietly closed behind the Bellow Brothers.

"How did you become the Boss of The Port City?" Clarke whispered, almost afraid to question her father.

"I don't know that there is an easy answer for that, Clarke. If I asked you how you became Mafietta, I don't know that you could give me a simple answer either."

Clarke let out a sigh, feeling she and her father hit a brick wall, but then he continued.

"When I was young, I didn't know who my father was at first. Momma worked hard, but she'd put Daddy out way before I was even born and he didn't start coming around regular until I was about 7 years old. I remember the first time he picked me up." Magnus smiled and continued with his chest stuck out as he described his father's car.

He was driving this shiny red Cadillac with leather seats, white wall tires, and an 8 track tape deck. He jumped out of the car in this burgundy zoot suit with his hair laid in small finger waves smiling, showing a gold tooth that peeked from the side of his mouth. He made me proud because nobody's Daddy on my block had a car. I began to stick my chest out too.

Then my momma came on the porch and I will never forget what she said to him, 'Porter Jones, if you take my son anywhere near anything illegal, this will be the last time you lay eyes on him and you can trust God that I mean what I say.' My Daddy just smiled. He knew that was my mother's way of saying hello. He had just gotten out of jail after a seven year bid. He and two of his homeboys robbed a bank just after my mom got pregnant and he got knocked, so his first stop after getting a big red car and brand new suit was on my mother's door step.

Why don't you come with us, Pearl? He asked. Momma knew this was coming because she had been getting ready all day, but she said, 'Nah Porter. I am gonna stay on here.' My daddy just laughed and finally made his way on the porch.

'Come on here, gal. You know I been waiting on you. Come on and introduce me to my son.'

My momma's face was filled with the biggest smile I'd ever seen as she swatted him away, BUT headed down the steps toward the shiny automobile.

For the next month, he earned my mother back. The beauty was that I got too see my mother fall in love with my father all over again. They were inseparable. Suddenly, Momma didn't have to work anymore and aside from us leaving town a couple times for Daddy to handle some business, it never hurt our family until one day when Porter wouldn't allow this young buck to sell on the Port City streets at all.

I'll never forget, the guy's name was Rico. He was the worst dope dealer ever and he was an even worse father. He sold weed to kids and that really rubbed my Daddy the wrong way. He wouldn't sell to him and he forbade any of the other pushers to sell to him either.

You see, Baby, hustlers used to have a code back in the day. They ain't worth a damn now, but anyway, this guy really had it in for Porter.

I was 16 years old and I came home one day and the house was super quiet with no dinner cooking. My mother always had dinner cooking or ready when the street lights came on. That was my cue to go check in at home. Then I remembered the strange blue car parked across the street. I stuck my hand in the vase by the door and pulled out Porter's nine millimeter. I place it behind my back and tipped to the porch where my momma made Porter take his visitors. I heard my mother screaming as the sound of the gun butt hit my father in the head, causing blood to fly against the wall.

I was only 16, but I wasn't afraid. I had to protect my family. I pointed the gun toward the coward's back and I fired two shots. Rico fell to the floor and I untied my parents. After that my father walked with a limp and within 10 years, he couldn't walk at all. Rico had shot him in the leg 3 times. That's when he asked me to take over. I did, but I always promised my father that I'd never let you know it and I'd always keep danger away from you.

He never wanted you to have blood on your hands. He wanted to build an empire for you. He wanted you to use his dirty money to find power and establish something great for our family. He loved you Clarke. He loved you from the time he first laid eyes on you and that was the price of business. You would always be shielded. I promised him this just before he kissed you for the last time and this is the way it has always been."

"So, Daddy, you are a second generation Boss?" Clarke asked.

'Well, I guess you can say that." Magnus answered, shocked at the question.

"Whew, that's a relief." Clarke laughed.

"What? I'm not sure that I follow you, Baby Girl." Magnus answered.

"This explains so much, Dad. I can't really explain it, but I've always had this secret desire to be a Boss. I am great leader and smart. Daddy and it used to make me so mad working for Eric and seeing all of the dumb ass mistakes drug dealers make. I always knew I could do it and get away with it. Working in the legal field helped make me smarter than them. Hell, I was smarter that Eric.

I gave him the winning arguments for some of the Port City's largest drug cases and he wouldn't even give me a raise. After that I knew it was time for a change and I wanted something kinda bad girl-ish. Now I know why. It's in my blood." Clarke answered laughing.

"I am not some alien. I am your daughter. That's why this works." Clarke stood up, the happiest she'd been since laying eyes on her little one. Thanks for spelling things out, Dad." Clarke kissed her father on the cheek and headed upstairs to check on her son.

Magnus laughed. That was his daughter all right and even though he hadn't told her – he was proud of who she'd become. He was proud of his Mafietta and if his father was here, he would be too.

6 STACKING THE DECK

"Why the hell is this bitch still alive?" Mandell screamed as he pounded the table with clenched fists.

No one at the table was willing to speak and incur the wrath of Mandell. He'd been impossible to be around since his brother, Hiram, was killed.

"So, all of you were there and no one has anything to say. Nobody can tell me why this bitch and her baby are still alive? Surely someone can tell me something." Mandell yelled.

He pulled a switch blade from his pocket and pressed its metal blade into Laz's throat. Julius sat at the other end of the table, watching his son-in-law's emotional rant. He'd allowed Mandell time to grieve, but now even his patience had grown short.

As blood began to drip from Laz's neck, Julius had enough.

"Put down the knife Mandell." Julius said.

"Nah, Pops. Somebody need tell me why Mafietta is still alive." Mandell said, pressing the knife even deeper into Laz's skin.

"Put down the damn knife." Julius ordered.

"Fuck that" was all Mandell could get out before a piercing pain ripped through his shoulder. The blade fell to the floor and Laz, taking advantage of the moment, turned and punched Mandell in the face. He fell to the floor.

Akmed rushed to Mandell's side. He was a doctor by trade and King by birth. His father and his father's father sat in his seat before him. They had the largest practice in the city and could easily funnel their profits through the firm.

Such was the case for everyone sitting at the table except Mandell. He was there by marriage and none of the other Kings respected that. They only humored him out of respect for Julius.

If Akmed had his way, Mandell would have been dead long ago. Julius knew the hot head had no place in the family, but he was determined to please his daughter and things had been hot and heavy for them ever since. Mandell needed to go and it was time Julius knew it.

Akmed put his feelings aside and bandaged the scar. Julius had only grazed the aspiring leader and he fell to the floor like a boy. He was no King. He was an imitation. Something must be done.

"Am I gonna live, Doc?" Mandell asked as Akmed taped down the bandage.

"Shut up, Stupid." Akmed said as he mushed Mandell in the face and walked back to his place at the table.

Julius released the group and met his old friend for a drink at his bar down the street.

❖

"Akmed, what am I gonna do with that fool?" Julius asked, shaking his head.

Akmed shook his head and chuckled to himself, "He should have been an accountant. This line of work isn't cut out for him."

"Tell me about it. If I let this hot head kill Clarke or her baby, we lose our access to the port or would surely have to go to war with her father. This thing is so much bigger than Mandell can see." Julius began to explain.

'What do you mean?" Akmed asked.

"Clarke sent me the video feed from the deal with that boy's brother and some mule named Dee. Their plan was to have Errol and his wife arrested so they could run The Kings. They'd even cut a side deal with a cop."

"What!?!" Akmed gasped.

"This mother fucker is bold, too. He decided that Hiram could report to him as Clarke does now and he could just take over the empire she's built. He had no idea they saw him coming and his lil dumb ass didn't know that Mafietta's daddy runs the East Coast either. We'd have to restructure everything if that door closes to us and this piece of shit is round her thinkin' he pullin' boss moves."

"Hell Nah, J. Those are corner hustler moves." Akmed returned.

"Exactly, but that's not even the half. Check this out." Julius said as he tossed a white business sized envelope.

Akmed could not believe his eyes as he glanced the photos.

"How could anyone be that disrespectful?" Julius asked.

"I don't know, Boss. How do you want to handle this?" Akmed asked.

"It's time we take a trip to the states." Julius returned.

"But you haven't been there in over 30 years. Are you sure you wanna head that way?"

"You damned right." Julius said feeling that old flame coming back. "It's time for an old fashioned sit down and besides, I want to finally meet this Mafietta. Then we can decide who will die."

Admiral ran from his office to Errol's study as soon as he got the news. He opened the door, winded and out of breath.

"What's wrong? Why are you running?" Errol asked.

"They're coming." He said nervously.

"Who's coming?"

"Akmed and Julius." Admiral said as a look of confusion covered his face.

"What!?! I can see Akmed, maybe. He comes out every year or so, but no one has seen Julius in like 45 years, right." Errol asked.

"No, boy. It's only been about 30." Admiral snickered.

"So why is he coming out now?" Errol probed.

"Get this. He wants to meet Mafietta and Magnus."

"What? How can he come to the Port City and overlook me like that? Clarke is my wife. I run the Port City Kings." Errol pouted.

You have to look at the big picture here if you want the clear picture. You have two fathers with their daughters thrown deeper in the life than they need to be because of the men they've chosen to marry. Magnus and Julius are more alike than you think.

Julius is no fool. He hasn't been untouched this long because he is unwise. He understands Magnus' importance to his business here. It seems your Mafietta may wield a bit more power than you knew, huh? Admiral joked.

"I guess you're right. I married into Hustler Royalty."

"Do you think they'll be able to dead the issue?" Admiral asked.

"If I know my wife, you'd better believe it." Errol smiled.

"Daddy, how did you get Julius to come out of those hidden hills?" Clarke asked.

"I have my methods." Magnus chuckled.

"Daaaaaaad!" Clarke pouted, bouncing baby Errol on her knee.

"Okay, okay. Just stop pouting." Magnus laughed. "Julius at his core is a family man just like me. He built his empire for his family, just like me. He planned to one day have his son take over. Only, he had a daughter."

"Just like you?" Clarke asked.

"Nope, you didn't have to be a man to run The Port City Kings or to triple its profits. I just wished you would have let me know a little earlier. You could have tripled my money." Magnus smiled.

"So where does Mandell fit into all of this?" Clarke asked still trying to get to the bottom of things.

"I can't really say right now, but sit back, Baby. This situation is about to get real interesting."

"How do you know they aren't coming to kill us all?" Clarke asked, holding her son a little tighter.

"Baby Girl, your Daddy never plays a game that isn't fixed." He winked at his daughter and went to talk to Errol and Admiral. He would need their help.

7 YOU'RE MY BITCH

Lena began to fall asleep as she listened to Mandell try to weasel his way out of this one.

"Baby, it wasn't my fault. Sheena was grinding up an me and before I could push her away, she kissed me dead in the lips and that's when you walked in." Mandell tried to explain.

"Uhmm hmmm" was all he seemed to be able to get from Lena. She wouldn't let on as to whether she believed him or not.

"You gotta believe me, Baby. I don't want nobody else but you." Mandell pleaded.

For the first time in their marriage, Mandell had lost her. He could only wonder what would happen next. If she or Julius ever found out that he tried to take over the Port City and cut the Kings out – he was a dead man and he knew it. Holding on to Lena was his only option right now.

Lena watched Mandell as he searched his mind for words. She actually enjoyed watching him squirm.

"Baby, don't you know better than some hood rat like Sheena. She can't hold a candle to you."

"I know that and you knew it too. It didn't stop you from pushing up on her though. I watched your drunk ass all over her and it's not the first time I've seen you in action either." Lena advised.

"Baby, I don't know what you're talking about." Mandell lied, hoping Lena was bluffing.

"I know all about your 6 month old in the states, just like I know about your plan to cut Julius out so your brother Hiram could run the Port City Kings and you could take over the East Coast drug trade. Did you think I wouldn't find out information about those closest to me?" Lena asked, getting annoyed.

"Baby, Lena. You don't understand."

"What is there to understand? I couldn't have children so you went out and found someone else to have one for you. You are foul on so many levels, so guess what Mandell." Lena continued. "You'd better get used to kissing my ass because you just became my new bitch. You bet on the wrong team this time, Dell. Now get a pillow and get the fuck out of my room before I start shooting."

Mandell wasted no time getting out of Lena's sight. She was a sure shot and he didn't want to be the next victim. For days Mandell walked around on egg shells waiting for his wife to talk to him. The morning finally came.

Mandell woke when Lena sat herself on top of him. Her neatly trimmed pussy was just inches from his face. He looked up to see Lena's open robe. Her breasts fell out of their covering to display hard nipples. Mandell could not stop the growing bulge coming from his midsection. He palmed Lena's ass cheeks with both hands and pulled Lena's landing strip closer to his mouth.

He stuck out his tongue and began to flick it back and forth against her closed lips. As they parted open, he flung his tongue into her softness. He licked back and forth and up and down until Lena began to moan. He knew his wife and despite his indiscretions, he knew how to please her.

Mandell began to slowly suck his wife's clit and juices began to flow from her insides, onto his lips, down his chin and onto his neck, but he didn't care. He'd hurt Lena and now it was time to make it all better. He let her happiness fall into his mouth and he pulled away to allow Lena to see him drink of her gift to him.

Lena quickly lifted her hand and slapped Mandell so hard he was stunned. Then she pushed his head down onto the armrest of the couch and sat on his face. She screamed as he plunged his tongue in and out of her hole. Mandell grabbed Lena's breast to steady his wife as he licked her walls. Her screams filled the room, and he readied himself to give her the –D- she needed.

He reached to grab his penis and Lena slapped him again.

74

"You're my bitch, remember." Lena laughed as she closed her robe and left her husband, his hard dick, and his bruised ego on the couch.

8 BABY COMES FIRST

Clarke dug her fingers into Errol's back. He let out a moan, stuck somewhere between pleasure and pain. As Clarke heard his reaction, she began to speed up her rhythm. Errol felt his wife's walls tightening around him. The warmth surrounded him like a glove and now it was his turn to come.

He flipped Clarke over and held on to her waist tightly, allowing more of him to enter her space. She threw her head back as he rubbed her depths. Suddenly that cold feeling was taking over her body and it felt great. She had an orgasm on the way.

Errol was kissing his better half passionately on the mouth, when a soft and familiar cry came from the other side of the room. Errol Magnus Bellow was wide awake and their personal party was over. Errol jumped up to run for Little EM as he was called, but Clarke stopped him.

"Boy, go somewhere and put your dick up. I don't want that thing hanging in my baby's face." Clarke joked as she got up to attend to the one person she loved more than anything.

EM's bright eyes looked up to Clarke as she came to rescue him from the confines of his crib. A smile soon spread across his face, exposing a toothless smile.

Clarke tied her robe and lifted her son from the crib. She could barely make it back to the bed before Errol entered with a warm bottle and a diaper in hand.

Clarke had to admit. Errol was an excellent father. When Sebastian, Errol's tailor, made his newest suit; he also had a matching one designed for his son. That made Clarke proud.

Errol reached for his son and in another swift movement, had EM's bottle in his mouth. The happy parents smiled as their son gulped the milk.

"It's hard to believe that someone tried to steal all of this from us. Clarke said, reflecting on the last three months. There are so many days that lead my thoughts to what could have been instead of what was. God was with my dumb ass that day." Clarke reminisced.

"From now on, Babe, you can't go anywhere without a tail. Black can stay with you and your Dad insists that one of his guys be with you as well."

"I get it, but I don't want this for our baby. What are we gonna do, send him to preschool with body guards or home school him just so I know he's safe? I won't be forced into a corner with my son. You gotta get us out of this Errol. I almost lost my baby once and I refuse to let that happen again. Call whomever you need to, but I want that damned Mandell. I want his head on a platter and I ain't bull shittin. If they can't make that right, then I am gonna tell my Daddy to close the port to them and nobody from The King camp will make any money. Most of all Mandell, and the real hidden hand, Julius." Clarke spewed as she worked herself into a fit of anger.

"Calm down, Babe don't let the little one see you so upset. Magnus has it all worked out. I am not sure of all of the logistics yet, but if he says he has it worked out, he does. You know your Pops." Errol pointed out objectively.

"Well, I am not sure what I could possibly say to Lena and Julius when they get here." Clarke responded, getting a little star struck but understanding the task at hand.

"Who knows?" Errol asked. "I'm sure you'll think of something fabulous."

"Yes, sure, Babe. I'll throw a party and then kill everyone there like they did on The Game of Thrones." Clarke joked.

Errol laughed and EM bounced up and down on Errol's lap mimicking his father. The brand new mother sat back smiling, in appreciation of her family. She whispered a quiet prayer for their safety.

'We gotta get out, Errol." Clarke said, changing the mood.

"I know, Babe." Her husband replied.

"We have more than enough money to clean this up and legitimize everything. If I had to pick, that would be the way to go." Clarke responded.

"What about the Kings?" Errol asked.

"What about them?" Clarke asked getting aggravated. "The silent head of The Kings tried to kill me. Think about what could have happened. Not only were they trying to kill me, they were trying to stamp out your legacy after everything you've done for the ungrateful bunch." Clarke complained.

"You have a point there." Errol remarked, actually taking a second to consider the flip side of this coin.

Little EM began to get fussy and Errol rose, taking his son into his arms and heading toward the window. He kissed his baby boy as a single tear fell from the face of a father onto his son.

"What if they resist the change?" Errol asked.

"Who cares?" Clarke asked "I am sure my father will make them an offer they can't refuse." Clarke responded talking in a raspy tone trying to sound like the Godfather.

Errol smiled, but his mind was racing. Clarke just may be onto something. Errol felt small hands on his face and he looked lovingly to his son.

"You are right, Clarke. I couldn't live if something happened to one of you and that crap at the hospital was too close of a call for me to ever fully trust the hidden hand of The Kings. Mandell went too far and even if he does apologize. He has to go." Errol responded.

Clarke laughed at her husband trying to sound all politically correct in front of his son who was just beginning to doze off again. He seemed to have loved the small spot he'd found on his father's shoulder to nestle his head in.

Clarke walked over to the window to kiss two of the most important men in her life.

"Family first." Clarke said.

"You're right, Babe." Errol agreed as he crossed the room to place EM back in his crib. "Baby comes first."

Clarke smiled and headed back to bed knowing Errol was finally ready to leave The Kings.

9 HOOD ROYALTY

Julius' arrival was nothing short of the scene from Coming to America when Akeem's parent's came to pick him up. He and Lena rode in a big body Black Mercedes Benz with 2 black Suburbans in front of and behind the main car.

The group flew onto a small private airstrip operated by some of the city's most elite. Hired guards were on hand, waiting for their arrival. Clarke, Errol, and Black sat in a black Suburban of their own watching the display of power and importance.

"Two big guys with dreds exited first. A short bald guy from the on the ground security team handed them both guns. Mandell exited first, followed by Akmed, Julius, Lena and two more guards.

"Dang." Clarke said. "They ain't even left the airport yet and they already strapped."

"Yep, don't you just love it?" Errol asked.

"Love it? Why would I love it? This just means there are four more people who can shoot us."

Black chuckled, trying not to laugh at his old friend.

"Do you see the short bald headed guy?" Errol asked.

"Yes. Why?" Clarke responded.

"Does he look familiar to you?"

"No." Clarke said, glancing the fellow.

"Look closer that's Mr. Flagg. He comes in once a week for the goat?"

"What is he doing here?"

"Black interjected now, "Clarke don't you know that man runs the largest legit gun shop and security firm in the city.

". . .and now he's working for Mandell and Julius? Clarke asked.

"Seemingly." Errol said with a smirk on his face.

"What do you mean seemingly?" Clarke questioned.

"Trust me, babe, he's with us. You can' do a lot with rubber bullets.

Errol tapped the back of the driver's seat and they headed to the Marley Grill to meet their distinguished guests.

Julius and Akmed were impressed. Magnus sure knew how to roll out the red carpet. The duo laughed as Akmed lit the spliff lying in the ash tray and Julius twisted the top of his Red Stripe Beer. The old friends were relaxed and ready to enjoy a rare visit to the states. Business would come later.

The Marley Grill was closed for a private party and the block that housed the restaurant was closed to outsiders. The suburban pulled up to a covered walk way that extended from the curb to the front door of the establishment.

"Nice touch." Julius remarked.

"Yep. They are keeping the hidden hand – hidden." Akmed answered as his door opened and he exited the luxury automobile. Lil' Stupid met Akmed as he exited. They exchanged a hidden hug and Steve, aka Lil' Stupid, handed his father a gun and this one had real bullets.

Akmed returned to the car for Julius and Lena.

Mandell's heart raced as they approached the Marley Grill. He hadn't been allowed to ride with Lena and her father. This could only mean they were on to him. His days were numbered and he knew it.

"Hey, Mason. You got an extra burner man?" Mandell asked, trying to get ahead of the next situation.

"Sure thing, Boss." The hired hand replied as he handed him a gun from Mr. Flagg's shop.

"You seem shook." Mason inquired.

"Nah, I just got a lot on my mind." He replied nervously.

"Time soon come to relax." Mason smiled.

"That's exactly what I'm afraid of." Mandell admitted, swallowing hard and wiping his brow.

The group had a very informal but hearty meal, enjoying a few laughs and talking about the latest football (soccer) tournament. After everyone was stuffed and had just had a slice of Admiral's famous rainbow cake, it was time to talk turkey.

Julius and Akmed left with Magnus and Errol. While Lena, Clarke, and Black left together in the next vehicle. Mandell looked around at Mason. His team had just left him. He held his composure as he met the questioning gaze of those left in the room. The heavy hitters were gone and Mandell was left here with the street team.

A smirk covered Mandell's face as he leaned to Mason. Two could play this game. If Lena was going to leave him like that; he was going to check on his family. He hadn't seen his daughter in months.

Mason pulled the car around and Mandell jumped in, intent on a day spent with his real family, not the one he pretended to be a part of with Lena. There was only a matter of time before he would be found out, but as with any other con-artist, Mandell was waiting on the big take. He'd messed things up with Hiram, but he had one more chance to bring the Kings to their knees and he was going to take it, right after he got Tesha and Edwina to a secure place.

10 IT'S LIKE THAT?

Tesha was always home and available anytime she knew Mandell was coming to the city and this time was no different. She'd just gotten her hair and nails done and she patiently sat on the couch watching her daughter play with the $100 robot dog her father sent just days before. She was happy. For the first time in months her family would be complete again.

Mandell told her he'd have to go back to the islands for a few months after his brother was murdered in a car explosion, but that was all she knew and being the kept woman she was, Tesha never asked questions. It didn't bother her that the man she loved was a bit of a ghost. He paid the bills and their beautiful Edwina wanted for nothing. She was Mandell's first child and he spared no expense.

Life was good and Tesha began to think it had just gotten better when she heard a knock at her door. She smoothed the wrinkles in her form fitting dress. Her island man loved to see her curves and she had them on display today just for him.

She picked up Edwina and rushed to the door to meet her man, but instead there were two tall men in dark suits.

"Ummm, Hello. May I help you?" Tesha asked through a trembling voice.

"Mam, Mandell is in danger and we need you to come with us." The tallest of the men spoke.

"What? What do you mean trouble? Why didn't he call himself?" Tesha asked getting even more nervous.

The other guy chuckled, "Mam, if he could have called you, then he wouldn't be in danger now would he?"

Tesha had to think fast on her feet. She knew these giants were not the type to take no for an answer.

"Hold on and let me grab my baby's diaper bag and a few more things. Won't you come in?"

"No Mam. We'd best stay out here." The other stranger answered.

Tesha closed her door and quickly grabbed the baby 380 in the vase by the door. She was mad at Mandell for putting a gun in her home with their small daughter, but he must have been able to forsee this kind of thing happening. She ran around quickly grabbing toys, milk, diapers, wipes, and gas drops for Edwina.

She stuffed the small burner into a side compartment of the diaper bag and she opened the door to meet her new chauffeurs.

"We're ready, gentleman." She said, determined to keep her composure.

The two men quickly rushed the mommy and daughter to an all-black Suburban with dark windows and shiny rims.

At least Mandell sent me some protection. Tesha thought, but she couldn't have been more wrong. Her beloved beau was just feet away on the other side of the street. He fought the initial reaction to yell to her when he saw Tiger and Jackal coming out of Tesha's brownstone.

These trained killers were former Special Forces guys and Lena's personal security. She only sent them out when shit was hot, so why in the world would they be taking his baby momma?

Suddenly, the picture became very clear for Mandell. Lena hadn't even given him the time to say hello to his daughter. All he could think as he slowly pulled behind the moving Suburban was – *Damn, it's like that??*

11 THE BED YOU MADE

Errol poured glasses of cognac as Magnus handed Akmed, Julius, and Admiral each Cuban cigars. He listened to the hearty laughs coming from men who sounded like old friends. Anna passed out the numbing liquid before closing the heavy oak door behind her and heading to the kitchen to prepare a snack.

"I can't tell you how sorry I am that your daughter was harmed, Magnus. That was a rookie move and it had nothing to do with any decision I made." Julius said before puffing on his cigar.

"I am just thankful that she and my grandson are alive and well." Magnus returned.

Silence fell over the room as two old friends were at a loss for words. The usual conversations just seemed so improper right now. Akmed broke the silence.

"Well, how is that grand baby of yours?" He asked.

For the first time since the men arrived, the tension was broken. It was almost as if Magnus was waiting on them to ask.

"Akmed, man he is so smart. He in only a few months old, but he can say words."

"Oh, stop it. That baby is too small to talk."

Magnus, happy to prove his friend wrong, pulled out his phone and scrolled through his line of videos to find the one of his grandson saying "woke up" as he woke up last week.

The crowd laughed at the video and the stillness returned.

"What do you want to do with him? Julius asked.

"Blood for blood." Magnus responded. "He had my baby shot and now I want him dead. I can't sit here and wait on him to pull something else. What did you have in mind?" He asked Julius.

"Makes me no never mind so long as you get him the hell away from my daughter. I am sick of the cheating son of a bitch and even though Lena won't tell me, I think she is too. Do you know that mother fucker had a baby on her."

"Damn. That's cold." Errol responded. "Doesn't he know that you never let the streets follow you home?"

"You could write a handbook with the shit this lil clown doesn't know." Akmed interjected.

"Anybody willing to literally blow up your East Coast connection is one of two things – enterprising enough to keep around or so dumb they don't deserve to breathe. Where does this clown fit in?"

Akmed laughed. "He doesn't' fit in. That's the problem. He's impulsive and hardheaded. If it wasn't for Lena, his ass would have been gone already."

"Yeah." Julius chimed in. "You know what it was like when her mom was killed, man. I can't put her through another loss."

"I'll bet her skin is thicker than you think." Akmed offered. "She'll check his ass when she has enough."

"Magnus, my Lena has gone Mafietta." Julius chuckled. "She had Jackal and Tiger go to this hoe's house and take the lady and her child to a hotel. She knows what Mandell is doing and if I know my daughter, I know that she can handle her own."

"What happened to our girls?" Magnus asked shaking his head.

"They took after their fathers." Julius laughed. "And now this ignant mofo has to sleep in the bed he's made. I will deal with Lena, Magnus. Do what you have to do."

"Great idea, Julius, but he's your guy, you should take care of him." Errol interjected.

"I hear ya, Youngblood. We got you. I just gotta protect my daughter. That's something you can relate to, surely, right? I need to get her mentally prepared to be without the clown." Julius said before gulping down his drink.

Lena fell back onto the couch as her body trembled. *This is the reason I can't let this man go.* She thought as she tried to control her breaths. Mandell stood to his feet and began wiping his chin with the pocket square that matched his tie. He walked over to the wet bar, washed his hands, and poured he and his wife a drink.

Lena wasted no time in letting the warm liquid roll quickly down her throat. She didn't even taste it. She didn't want to. She just needed the courage to have her mind take control and do the things her heart could not.

"Slow down." Mandell said lovingly to his wife.

"Really, Dell? Are you giving a fuck about me today?" Lena asked sarcastically.

"What do you mean?" He asked.

"Don't play with me asshole. I am just like my father. I don't ask a question I don't already know the answer to." Lena said, feeling her strength come.

"What do you want me to say Lena?" Mandell asked, tired of being stuck between the women he loved.

"I want you to say that she fucks you better, or that she has a root on you. Say something that will make me feel better, you mother fucker. You made one of the richest women on the east coast feel like nothing. Money couldn't keep you in my bed. Cars, a fucking name in the streets, none of it was good enough for you was it? You still had to have your whore?"

"Why do you have to call her a whore? It wasn't her fault Lena. It was mine."

E. W. BROOKS

Mandell felt something warm and wet splash his face suddenly as he realized Lena had thrown the rest of her drink in his face. He instinctively grabbed her arms. Lena shook her shoulders to rid herself of his grasp, but Mandell would not let go. It was Lena's turn to get a dose of her own medicine.

"I am sick of you walking around here pretending to be so fucking innocent when you're hands aren't clean either Lena. Who is Arthur Blane?"

"What are you talking about?" Lena asked.

"Do you think I don't know that you've been skirting around town with that big muth fucka. I hear it so much it makes me sick and you won't stop either. You are just all out with it and every time some clown ass steps to me, they say some slick shit because of the stuff you're out there doing In the street, I have to deal with the bullshit. I've never disrespected you that way. I kept my bullshit far from home."

"Was that your way of rationalizing the shit? I don't care what you met in the street, your vow was to me and it never should have happened. Your dumb ass couldn't buy common sense if it were for sale." Lena said before spitting in his face.

Mandell had enough. He pushed his wife down onto the couch and he began to slap her. First on the left side of her face, then on the right. She opened her mouth to scream, but he grabbed her by the throat. She tried to call out for Tiger or Jackal but the words wouldn't come out. She could feel her breaths becoming shallow.

She kneed Mandell in his crotch and for a second as he moaned, he loosened his grip. That was all Lena needed. She screamed, "Jackal!"

The door burst open and Tiger and Jackal beelined straight for Mandell. He threw his hands in the air screaming, "I'm sorry, Lena. I'm sorry. Please forgive me. Please don't let them hurt me."

Jackal, who now saw Lena as a little sister, was furious. He rushed Mandell and threw him up in air as if he were a paper weight. As his body fell to the floor, Tiger pummeled the adultering abuser's face.

"STOP!" Lena screamed.

Tiger immediately paused with his fist just inches away from Mandell's nose.

"Pick him up." Lena instructed. The duo did as they were told. Each man held one of Mandell's arms as that sat him on his knees.

Lena's eyes scanned the room as she looked for something rock hard to hit this fool with. Her eyes settled on Clarke's Lalique black and crystal Tourbillions Vase. She walked over to the $9,200 object and was surprised by its weight. Not only was it beautiful and made of heavy crystal, there were streaks of platinum in it too.

"Get him on his feet." Lena instructed.

Jackal and Tiger grimaced as they watched Lena rear back with the weighty piece of crystal and head straight for Mandell's balls.

He let out a gut wrenching scream as the crystal vase hit his scrotum like a Mack truck. Lena recognized this sound and could immediately relate. She'd let out the same painful cry when she found out about Little Edwina, Mandell's daughter.

Lena repeated her actions twice more as Mandell screamed for his life.

A look of relief crossed his face as Black and Akmed entered. Instead of them rushing to assist, they began to laugh.

"It's clear, Boss." Black yelled through the door and Maguns, Julius, Errol and Admiral rushed into the room.

"What in the world are you doing, baby?" Julius asked, unsure of what he was seeing.

"Well, Dad, it appears that my husband doesn't know what to do with his private parts, so I figured he didn't need them."

Julius walked toward his daughter intent and taking the vase and sending Mandell to be watched at a local hotel while he and Magnus ironed out their wrinkles and solidified their continued hold on the Eastern Seaboard.

Instead, he saw his daughter's red face. There were the beginnings of a bruise on both her cheeks. His eyes fell to her throat as he saw clear hand prints. He stuck to his first mind and took the crystal vase from his daughter, but he didn't return it to its place on the table as he'd planned.

He lifted the vase a couple times as if it were a weight to gauge it's real weight.

"Lena, you did good, Baby. This thing weighs about 15 pounds."

"Thanks, Daddy." Lena replied with a smile. She knew it was over for Mandell now and for the first time since he'd stolen her heart, she didn't care.

He drew his arm back so quickly that Mandell missed it but he soon felt the results of Julius' actions. He could barely stand as a piercing pain covered the right side of his face. Blood began to ooze from his face and that's when Lena had seen enough.

She walked over to her father and placed her hand on his raised arm.

"Please, don't do it Daddy. I have something really special lined up for my husband. He wanted an American whore and now he has one and a bastard child. Let's not take a man from his family. He wanted a life here, let's make sure he has it."

Julius looked at his daughter confused by her words, but for now he went along with her charade. He knew how dramatic his daughter could be, so despite his indiscretions, Julius felt a little sorry for the boy because he had no idea what Lena's wrath was like.

Magnus stood back with his arms crossed as he watched the show. That little forked tongue, fake ass hustler was finally getting what was coming to him. Errol looked at his father-in-law with admiration. *Magnus is the man. Damn I married into a banging ass family.* He thought as he and Admiral watched the fireworks.

"Why are you letting them do this to me?" Mandell asked as he pleaded to Lena for his life.

"Mandell, no one else will ever touch you, but you will sleep in the bed you made." And with that Lena St. James headed towards the door.

"Daddy, don't kill him." She said over her shoulder. "I have plans for him."

She smiled as the closed the door, leaving the man to whip his ass. The team didn't' take kindly to men abusing women and she knew it. Mandell was gonna have a long day.

12 GIRL POWER

Clarke was using Google Hangout to chat with her mother and talk to EM. She missed her son, but knew it was best that he not be around for this kinda thing. Then, she heard the knock that she'd known would be coming. The sound was too soft to be a man and it wasn't Anna's musical knock. *Oh, here we go.* She thought. It's Lena.

"Momma, I gotta go. Kiss me baby for me. Talk to you soon, man" Clark said to the little man she missed so much and she hit the red receiver to end the call as she yelled, "Come in" in the direction of her door. Clarke rushed to Lena's side as she saw her bruised face.

"Oh. Lena. I'm so sorry. What happened to you?" Clarke asked with genuine concern.

"I pushed him too far and he snapped." Lena responded.

"That mother fucker put his hands on you?" Clarke asked, trying to hold her composure.

Lena fell into Clarke's arms. "I don't know what to do Mafietta. I love this dog so much, but he keeps biting me. I feel like such a fool. What do I do?" Lena asked, sobbing uncontrollably.

Clarke led Lena over to the overstuffed love seat by the window and she held her new friend as she cried. There was no Mafietta in this room. Instead, there was two women connecting through tears, hugs, and unspoken experiences. When Lena had no more tears she sat up smoothed out her clothes.

"I'm sorry to lay all of this at your door, but it is time to deal with the truth of my situation. Living in the lie of it only made things worse. How do I deal with this asshole and maintain some level of pride. I am the daughter of a King. This can't go unpunished. It will make me look weak. How do you decide when to pull the trigger?"

"I only pull the trigger when I know that turning my back would make it a target for someone's bullet." Clarke replied. She wanted to stay as objective as possible.

"Dell has the best dick I've ever had. There is something about the wind in his hips that hit spots that I didn't know were there before. He made me rain and I never wanted to give that up."

Clarke chuckled, "You're taking all of this shit because of the D?"

Lena had to laugh as well. "I guess I do sound like some maniac, but I love this man. I married late and before then I had only been with 3 men. I was 35. It's hard to date when your father is Julius St. James, but there came Mandell. He had this big smile and a quiet confidence that drew me in. He seemed so together. Daddy had him checked out and things were cool, so we started dating. Mafietta, he was the perfect gentleman. I couldn't wait for him to touch me, but he didn't rush. He took his time with me. He made me wait 3 months, like in that Steve Harvey book. I was pissed because we'd petted pretty heavy a couple times and I could see the size of the man I'd be dealing with. I was ready for the challenge, but it finally happened on Valentine's Day and it was the most amazing sex of my life. I was done after that."

"How could you base a decision about marriage on something as whimsical as sex?" Clarke asked.

"Easy. What can anyone do for us that we can't pay to have done ourselves? How can they be respected as the provider when they could never provide the way our fathers do? How daunting is that for a man? My father owns islands. He could never compete, but he could make my body tremble in ways I couldn't, even with my platinum membership to Club ZZZZZ."

"What's Club ZZZZZ? Girl, it's amazing. They're erotic stores that use different sex toys each quarter. The stories tell you how to use them and what it felt like using them for the first time with their partner. You have to check them out. They're amazing. I even have one in my suit case right now."

"Are you serious?" Clarke asked.

"Yes. That's it. I am sending the latest one to your phone right now. What's your email?" Lena asked as she grabbed the Samsung Note from her Alviero Martini handbag.

Clarke gave Lena her email and within minutes her phone was beeping with the book.

"That was fast." Clarke laughed.

"Girl, this Amazon Kindle thing is the truth, but how did we get way over there. I thought we were talking about Mandell."

"Oh, yeah. We were, but then I went off on this sex toy tangent. My point was that I had tried everything and nothing made me feel as good as I did with Mandell."

"So, you let him cheat on you because you're whipped?" Clarke asked as she tried to hide her growing annoyance with this entire conversation.

"No, Clarke, It is much more involved than that. I let him cheat because I don't know what it feels like to do someone else's dirty work and then feel so dirty that you need someone's bed to feel like a man again. Do you have any idea how many bodies Mandell has on him? Fifteen, Clarke. I think that would make it challenging for anyone wanting to feel normal. I know that Tesha girl was his way to come home and feel some type of normalcy even if it is a lie."

"Lena, you can give him a pass if you want. It's your relationship and no one has to approve its decisions but you two. It's all about what your heart can hold and what you can sleep with at night, but I will say that I never pegged you as the open marriage type."

"I didn't either, but what do you do when you love a rolling stone?" Lena asked, searching her friend's eyes for answers.

"You don't have to decide anything right now. Maybe you should give yourself some time." Clarke suggested.

"If you can say that, you don't know my father. He likes swift justice. In fact, he demands it." Lena said as her voice trailed off to a whisper.

"I don't think it's necessarily right to kill a man because he doesn't love you the way you love him." Clarke said, "but it is more than fair to slaughter a man who hired someone to have you killed."

"What do you mean?" Lena asked.

"Your husband has been very busy. He knows you have Tesha and Edwina and he has hired someone to kill you if he finds they've been hurt."

"How would YOU know something like that?" Lena asked.

Clarke walked over to her computer and pulled open a file with Mandell's name on it. One of the many files was labeled T and E Protection. She double clicked on the video and her husband began to speak.

"Make sure you hear me right man, I love my wife but I love my baby momma too and I can't have one putting the other in danger. You feel me?" He asked the tall freckled faced curly haired man in the black trench coat.

"I got you, so I wait to hear from you and if you give the word, I dead Lean St. James."

"That's about the size of it."

"I hope you know what kinds of curses you're about to pull out of this box by messing with these people." The mysterious man offered.

"I got this. You just do what I've paid you to do." Mandell said before giving the man two banded stacks of hundred dollar bills.

Lena couldn't believe her eyes and ears. After everything she'd done for him, how could he do this to her? It wasn't enough that he'd had a child with someone else knowing that she could never give him one; he continued to place this new family's needs before hers. She was gonna fix his ass.

Emotional decisions made for some of the worst ones, but Clarke was curious.

"If you could do whatever you wanted to do to Mandell; what would it be?" Clarke asked and for the next 30 minutes she listened to one of the most intricate and decisive plans she'd ever heard. Once Lena laid out the details, Clarke knew she would need to business with this woman, but for now they were going to enjoy whipping Mandell's ass.

Lena was giving this clown everything he wanted.

13 I TOLD YOU – YOU'RE MY BITCH

Clarke spent the rest of the afternoon being project manager to Lena's plan for Mandell. She was pounding away at the keyboard when Errol came into her office.

"Hi Babe." Clarke said, eyes focused on the computer screen.

"You will never guess what kind of day I had." Errol said as he fell into the Marcella Leather Chaise Lounge beside Clarke's desk.

"I just saw a grown man get his ass whipped like he was a 10 year old child."

"You can't mean they really whipped him?" Clarke snickered.

"Yep, that's exactly what I mean. Julius took off his belt and beat his bare ass until he got tired, then he handed the belt to me."

"He did what?" Clarke asked. "Did someone hold him down? I know he didn't just lay there and let y'all beat him like that."

"Oh, yes he did. That's all you can do when you know you're wrong. No one had to hold him down. His guilt did that."

"So, did you beat him with that belt, Babe?" Clarke asked, sure her husband would say yes.

"Nope."

Clarke jumped from her seat to the chaise lounge and pummeled Errol in his chest.

"What do you mean, nope? This nigga shot me and could have killed our son and you did nothing?"

Errol placed his forefinger over Clarke's moving mouth. When she finally closed it, he spoke.

"I let Black do it." Errol laughed as his words finally registered with his wife. "He had more stamina than I would have."

"I would have loved to see that." Clarke laughed as she imagined the scene.

"What did it feel like to see your wife finally vindicated and this clown was treated like the dog he is?" Clarke asked as she switched to Mafietta mode.

"At first, I was a little repulsed to see a grown man lie on the floor and scream like that, but then I considered the weeks you lay in the hospital as I watched you replay some of the most horrible times of your life and by the time Black was done welling on him. I really felt sorry for the brother. Who wants to wake in the morning as a man and then be reduced to nothing by the end of the day?"

"What is Julius going to do with him now?" Clarke asked.

"Give him to Lena." Errol answered.

"Uh oh. Let me tell you about my afternoon, then." Clarke watched Errol's face as she recounted Lena's plan.

"Well, it's a little dramatic of course and I shudder to hear of any man's manlihood being tampered with, but they could kill him instead."

Errol laughed as he thought of the hard, well – not so hard days Mandell had coming. *There is no need to take his life*. Errol thought. *The hell on earth Lena is creating for him is far worse.*

Julius and Akmed could not believe their ears as they heard Lena's plans for her husband and while it was a little more dramatic a gesture than he was used to, it worked.

"Daddy, why are you laughing? I know this all sounds crazy, but despite how pissed off I am at Mandell, it could never make me so bitter as to harm a child. Looking at the big picture means accepting that he did not do right by me, but allowing him to be a father to his little Edwina."

"Edwina, huh? You know her name?" Julius asked.

"I did my research. She's not quite two yet and she has the most beautiful eyes. That hood booger she has for a mother is a different story." Clarke said, trying to hide her anger. Julius always taught her it was a sign of weakness.

The thing he did encourage was knowing your opponent well before they know you. This wise father taught Lena to size up a man in 3 minutes based on his outfit, shoes, and first few minutes of conversation and up until Mandell, it had served her correctly. Her heart was in pieces lying on the floor and as everyone was going on with their life, she was left to face the fact that she loved a man who didn't love her back.

What were the alternatives? Lena knew that if she didn't handle Mandell, Errol and Clarke would and it would be permanently. Regardless of all he'd done, she still loved him and she wouldn't stand to see him hurt.

"I talked it over with the guys and the plan is solid. I've even picked up the salt-peter you asked for." Jackal reported.

"Great guys. Thanks. It's finally time Mandell got a dose of his own medicine." Lena said as she tried to mask her hurt.

"I'm exhausted now and we have a lot going on in just a few hours, so I need to catch some shut eye.

Lena kissed her father and Uncle Akmed and headed to the spacious bedroom that would be hers for the next few days.

When the door closed behind her, Akmed looked to his friend.

"Julius, that's a damned good plan. Maybe we should let Lena be more active in the organization?" He joked.

"Yeah, Yeah, Yeah." Julius laughed. "You leave my daughter out of this."

Lena couldn't help doubling back to the garage to see her husband once more before giving him his due and finally letting him go.

Her heart dropped as she saw the love of her life's swollen ass. He was lying face down on the floor with his pants just under his buttocks.

"What happened to you?" Lena asked, hiding all of her emotions.

"The Port City Kings happened. " Mandell replied curtly. "Your Daddy's gang beat me up. They're gonna kill me aren't they?"

"It's up to me and I haven't decided yet." Lena answered.

"Don't let them kill me, Baby." Mandell pleaded, but his words fell on deaf ears. Lena was fed up.

"I promise I won't let them kill you, but you are gonna be with that woman and her daughter, day in and day out. You wanted that life and now you can have it, permanently." Lena added.

Mandell knew this offer was too good to be true, even if it did sound good.

"What is the catch?" Mandell asked.

"Oh, that nasty little thing." Lena asked as she prepared herself to Mandell's reaction to her plans for him.

"I'm having you castrated." Lena said before pausing to gauge Mandell's reaction.

"Castrated!?! You can't do no shit like that, I have to go to the doctor to get it done and then I'll call the police."

"Boy, money makes the world go round and we have plenty of it, so Dr. Weaver is doing your surgery, but don't worry he is the best in the city."

"So what am I supposed to do with my balls cut off?" Mandell said, sure to himself that Lena was lying about his fate.
"I don't care what you do, Mandell. I'll just sleep better at night knowing that at least you won't be fucking anybody else. It's like I said, you're my bitch." Lena said as she headed to the door. She could hear her husband trying to loose himself from the rope he was tied in. She laughed at his efforts.

"Save it. You're stuck Baby." Lena said, closing the garage door and finally heading off for her nap.

14 FINALLY, ACCEPTANCE

Lena had no idea how tired she was as her head hit the pillow. Her body needed to rest and she fell right off to sleep. She tossed and turned as dreams of she and Mandell together consumed her. The thoughts of him touching her body, even in her dreams, pleased and repulsed her at the same time. She couldn't understand what her attraction was to this man and her subconscious mind was not sharing its secrets just yet.

Lena's nap ended with a start. She was arguing with Tesha, Mandell's baby momma, when she pulled a small pistol from her diaper bag. As she and her husband's side chick tussled for the gun, Mandell is just standing there pointing a gun in the direction of the quarreling women, trying to decide which of his women he'll shoot and which one he will protect. As Mandell's gun goes off, Lena feels a sharp pain in her shoulder as she falls to the ground."

Lena's fall felt so real that the pain transferred itself from her dream to her body as she began to scream in anguish. She felt like she was falling and she felt her hands flailing in the air she tried to save herself. She woke to a start. Tiger was knocking at the door.

"Yes. Who is it?" She asked, trying to regain her composure and shake this nasty nightmare she'd just had.

"Tiger, Mam. It's time." He reported.

Lena jumped out of bed, now even more determined to do what she had to do to be rid of Mandell forever. Her dream had been clear and while a small part of her wanted her estranged husband to do right by she and their marriage; the truth is that she knew better. Her dreams never lied and this time they'd just revealed that not only would Mandell choose the hood rat, he'd try to off her in the process. Lena wiped the tears that fell from her face as she considered the bleak possibilities her marriage held.

She grabbed the plush Egyptian cotton bath set and headed in the adjoining room for a shower. Lena needed to stand there and have the water wash away her pain. As the steaming hot water from the shower hit Lena's body from four different directions she closed her eyes and pretended that one of them was her husband, caressing her ass, one last time.

Lena lay against the wall of the shower and opened her legs as she positioned herself on the bench and enjoyed the steady and powerful stream of water that massaged her button. She bit her lip as she imagined Mandell doing that to her again. Nectar dripped from Lena's core as she imagined reuniting with her husband. Many women had forgiven infidelity. She would be in good company.

As imagined the best love she'd ever had, entering her body; she let her imagination completely take over. She could feel soft arms around her and strong legs that supported her full frame and lifted her up and down, over and over again on the best ride of her life.

As Lena climaxed, she was overwhelmed by a sharp pain in her chest. Just as in the dream, Lena felt like she was falling, except this time she was. She opened her eyes as her body hit the hard shower floor.

That was it, Lena couldn't deny the truth anymore. Mandell would always be able to send her into the throws of passion and make her cum like no other, but he could never be trusted. Lena realized how short sighted she'd been. She hadn't even considered the horrific things he'd done to Mafietta and her family and those incidents hadn't even been addressed.

Suddenly, Lena realized that he wasn't hers to deal with at all. Mandell's fate ultimately rested with the decision of The Kings. She would withhold her vote this time. The scorned wife had no problem with others handling Mandell, but she wanted no part of it. She had enough to work through without adding the weight of his death to her mounting pile of troubles.

She had to speak to Mafietta before she left. She would have her fun with Mandell, but he belonged to her new friend after.

15 THE BIG PICTURE

Magnus and Julius were alone for the first time since his arrival. They leaned back into their wide back chairs and for the first time in years, Magnus pulled a cigar from his pocket.

"Did you really?" Julius asked.

"Yep. I said my next Cuban spliff would be with you to celebrate millions and that time is now. We made it old friend." Magnus said before pulling on the fattie.

He inhaled its smoke and began to choke as he passed the bud of understanding to Julius.

"I heard about Lena's plans for Mandell. The apple doesn't fall far from the tree does it?" Magnus joked.

"I guess not." Julius had to laugh.

"I'll never forget that shit, man. You held that girl over the 13th floor balcony. She was shaking like a leaf. It took me 20 minutes to convince her that you wouldn't kill her."

"Those were the good old days, Magnus. Most folk were honest and business was somewhat fair, but now people want to shake your hand just to get close enough to stab you in the face. Back in the day you whipped a man's ass every day until somebody got tired and relented. Now you can whip a young buck and then he come back with a damned pistol." Julius shook his head and inhaled.

"I don't play with these young bucks out here, Man. I have to run a pretty tight ship around here to keep the powers that be, off my back. As long as the body count stays low or non-existent, they'll stay off my back. I had to make a few examples back in the day, but I'm fair out here, so I always had the respect of the street. Then y'all came." Magnus laughed, as Julius choked on smoke.

"Real talk, man – give it to me straight. What is going on with Mandell? What are y'all gonna do with him? That clown shot my daughter and his head's gotta roll."

"I know, Mag. These last few months have been hard for Lena. She didn't think I knew it, but she's been spying on her husband and found out all kinda shit. She found about him trying to set Errol up, him sending someone to kill Clarke, and to take the cake; this fool had a whole damned family throwed up in The Keys out on the 17th Street Extension."

"He should have known better. Women are better detectives than most real ones. Just think, if a woman had a finger printing machine, a DNA thing, and some surveillance equipment – oooh weeee. So that's why she was pounding his nuts with that heavy ass vase?" Magnus asked.

"Yep. I wanted to go grab her arm. She's heavy handed and I grimaced every time she hit the fool."

"I know, right. I don't like the guy, but I don't think he has to worry about having any more babies." Magnus laughed as he blew smoke from his mouth.

"She's not even done with him. By the time she is, I think he'll be ready to die." Julius said reaching for the blunt.

"We'll give him to the Kings when she's done. We haven't talked about it yet, but Lena knows the code and she knows what's coming."

"She and Clarke seem to get along very well. I don't doubt that they'll work things out." Magnus returned.

"Some good bud can always center a conversation, but check this out. Who would have thought that at the end of the day, our daughters just as capable as any man to run this thing."

"I know right, but you know if Clarke has her way, she'll be getting us out of the drug game completely."

Magnus watched as his friend took a long pull on the "proverbial" peace pipe.

"I don't know about that one, Magnus. What could we do that could net us the kind of money we make now?"

"I know it sounds crazy, but Clarke has a ton of ideas. Do you know that each of the Kings is a millionaire just from money that she skimmed from their cut. When you look at it, she set up each of them with a damned 401-k plan. No one has a reason to be mad if we dissolve because everybody has cake."

"I hear that, but I want legacy money. If Lena can spend it in two lifetimes, it isn't enough. I want the income Mandell. I support half of that island with my payroll and I can't just pull out the city's infrastructure like that. I have to find a profitable way to keep those families working and not for those poverty wages either. Tell your daughter if she can work that out, she has a deal." Julius decided.

The two men shook hands and decided to play a round of golf while their children had some fun.

"Do you think the girls will be okay without us?" Julius asked as he began to worry about Lena.

"Hell Yeah. They have our entire team and guns full of rubber bullets. They're just going to target practice."

The two old timers laughed and headed to Echo Farms for some sun, some liquor, and good times on the green.

16 DREAMS DO COME TRUE

Lena readied herself for Mandell's day of reckoning. There was no redemption from here. She shook her head to dispel the thought and her mind moved back to Mafietta. She had to holla at a fellow Boss before going any farther.

"Come in." Clarke said as she sat at her desk sending out emails.

"Hi Mafietta." Lena said.

"Hi, Nice Lady. What's up?" Clarke asked.

"Hey, I just wanted to speak to you real quick before I left. Do you have a minute?"

"Sure thing. Have a seat." Clarke said as she motioned to the seat in front of her desk.

"Thank you for allowing me to lose my mind in your arms. They're right. Heavy is the head that wears the crown." Lena tried to make light of the situation.

"No worries. We have to stick together. Men always do."

Lena looked her new friend in her eyes as she reached for her hand. Clarke admired the gesture and met her half way.

"I owe you an apology." Lena said as she squeezed Clarke's hand.

"Why?" Clarke asked with a puzzled look on her face.

"I was so wrapped up in my own feelings that I never considered yours. "My husb," Lena paused "No, Mandell tried to have you murdered. If anyone deserved vengeance, it was you. I was so blinded with hurt that I didn't stop to think and for that, I'm sorry."

"Lena, thank you, but I knew we'd double back to this conversation. They may call me Mafietta, but I am a woman first and I can relate to what you feel. I wanted to help a sistah going through. Business will come later. We have the rest of the week to map out Mandell's future, but thanks for mentioning it. I know with the skills you have, we can really make our legitimate mark in the world."

"I agree, but for now, my world dominance begins with handling my cheating, woman beating husband. I still can't believe that mofo put his hands on me, but I get it now. That's been my problem. I see things with my heart and the downside to that is it sees things as it wishes they were. It always gives someone an undeserved benefit or unwarranted second chance, but let's say that opening your eyes, especially the 3rd one can sometimes be a little overwhelming."

"Do you have three eyes?" Clarke asked Lena.

"In some things." She admitted. "but the truth is always in my dreams."

"Mine, too." Clarke said. She knew this was a true dynamic duo. "I know you gotta go, but call me if you need me."

"Sure thing. Can't wait to recap." Lena said as she rose to face her future and step into her own form of Mafietta.

On the other wing of the house, Jackal threw a fresh new suit on Mandell's bed, atop the bathroom set. Get dressed. You're going to see Tesha and Edwina. For the first time since his brother was killed, Mandell was afraid. Women were a dime a dozen but his daughter was the last extension of his blood line. He would take out every King and their entire families if someone harmed his child.

Mandell entered the adjoining bathroom and closed the door.

"No closed doors." Jackal yelled from the other side.

Mandell obliged. He would do whatever he had to do to see his daughter.

The water burned as it hit his open wounds. The bleeding finally stopped, but his eyes and lips were still swollen and his crotch was still extremely sore from its beating as well. The water simply reminded him of the abuse he'd suffered at the hands of his beautiful wife.

How crazy does that sound? Mandell thought to himself as he laughed. This woman just pounded my crotch with a crystal vase and I still think she's beautiful. He thought back to the good times with Lena. He loved her with all his heart. He never meant to stray from his marriage, but then there was Tesha.

Mandell remembered his first kill like it was yesterday. One of Errol's rivals was recruiting a new gang that was up to no good and they had to be handled to maintain the balance The Kings depended on to do business.

He went to Wrightsville Beach's Blue Water Grill to have a drink by the water. Hoping that taking a stroll and a long swim in its saltiness would wash away his sins. Tesha watched him as he fought the waves like a maniac. He allowed the water to beat his body and he seemed a bit more relieved each time the water covered his head. Tesha watched in fear, afraid that the water would swallow him up and never let him go, but it seemed the swimmer had enough. He walked from the water, obviously tired from his bout with Mother Nature.

That's when she knew she had to have him. She watched him rinse off at the pavilion on Johnny Mercer's Pier before disappearing into the souvenir shop. Tesha's heart throb emerged looking like a tourist for sure. His ugly outfit didn't cover the Figaro link necklace or bracelet he was wearing. This cat had cake and Tesha was ready to enjoy dessert.

She watched this new face enter Pier 21. They made great drinks and their flounder was the best in town, so

Tesha had nothing to lose by having a great dinner and hopefully landing some great sex and a new sugar daddy.

Tesha had seen his type before, overworked and undersexed. She knew how to bag this one and it wouldn't' take long. She potted Mandell at the bar and decided to make her move. She sat one chair away from Mandell and began by making small talk. After 3 rounds of drinks, he was spilling his guts. She didn't know what this man had done, but his conversation made it obvious that he was searching for some way to feel better and the rest is history.

Tesha copped a hotel room right on the beach and Mandell took out all of his frustrations on her willing body as he attempted to skeet all of his wrong doings into someone else's dark hole. Tesha mistook the exchange as this Mandingo man wearing her out. His goal was to get off and get gone. He couldn't believe the surprise when she popped up pregnant a month later, putting every career move he'd ever made in jeopardy.

Mandell could have denied his daughter or even forced Tesha into an abortion, but he decided against it. He chose to be a man and an example for his seed. He owed it to her and as time passed they settled into a bit of a routine and he would spend as much time with his accidental family as he could.

As crazy as it was, it never changed his love for his wife and his first goal was to always protect her and her feelings, but he'd done a horrible job and now he had to face the music, even if it meant his life.

Mandell thought back to Lena If only he could make her understand. She'd been nothing but good to him and it was his indiscretions and hot headedness that put him in this situation to start with. He imagined her forgiving him and finally allowing him into her soft and sweet body again.

He thought of Lena as he moved his hands back and forth using the friction of the soap to simulate his wife's wetness. He sped up the motion as he imagine his petite wife sitting on his big member and making his toes curl like she used to. He imagine her firm breasts in his mouth as his hands sped up.

Mandell begin to grunt when the shower door opened. It was Lena. His wife smiled as she watched him explode all over the shower wall. Normally he would have been satisfied, but as he had his last real audience with his soul mate, he continued to stroke his piece as her mouth watered.

Lena could never deny their attraction for each other and this moment was no different. She slowly peeled of her skirt and folded it neatly on the chair that sat in front of the vanity mirror. She turned around and bent over to remove her thong, making sure Mandell had a pristine view.

He stroke himself faster as he enjoyed the show. In one swift move, Lena turned and positioned herself on the counter. She lifted one leg in the air as she removed her stiletto and dropped it to the floor. She repeated the action with her other shoe before sitting on the counter with a pose that matched an old school Lil' Kim poster.

She licked her finger and began to rub her hand back and forth against her box. Mandell's grip tightened as he imagined being inside his wife again.

"Come here." Lena ordered.

Mandell, recognizing the opportunity to please his wife, stepped out of the shower and fell to his knees. He plunged his tongue into Lena's dark hole and licked its walls while his hand massaged her clit. He watched as Lena rested her head on the mirror and enjoyed his performance.

He switched and began to suck her clit as if his life depended on it as his pointer finger circled and massaged he walls. It had been months since Lena had been penetrated and he could tell. His dick throbbed and then Lena surprised her husband.

She grabbed his throbbing pleasure stick and quickly slid a condom onto her cheating husband's dick. She needed to feel him one more time and then she could move on. Maybe she would make him her love slave and what if he really wanted to change. Lena smiled as she considered the endless opportunities and felt the painful pleasure of her husband's huge dick parting her tight opening.

Mandell didn't rush at all. He took time penetrating her. He hadn't felt this in months and he suddenly realized why he'd always loved Lena. She never gave his pussy away, even when he was in the street trippin. He was wrong to accuse her.

He lifted his wife, member still deep inside her, breast in his mouth and he slowly grinded against her surfboard. Lena let out a small moan. Oh, how she loved Mandell's slow stroke. Mandell saw her reaction and remembered the way his wife like to be loved and he carried her willing body to the bed.

Lena loved the way Mandell was making her feel. His sex had her high and once again she considered a way to save her husband from the calamity of everything he'd done. She knew Clarke would understand her wanting to keep the vow to her husband. He would just have to redeem himself with The Kings instead of giving up his life.

Lena trembled as he stroked her spot. He knew just where it was and he wasn't letting up. Mandell sped up as Lena covered her face with a pillow to muffle the sounds coming from her mouth. Mandell made no effort to hide his moans. He wanted Lena to know just how good she made him feel.

I can explain everything that happened with Tesha and she'll forgive me. We can start over. Mandell thought to himself as he exploded in the condom inside his wife. He held onto Lena for dear life. Her decision could determine whether he would live or die so he had to make her understand.

Lena allowed Mandell to hold her as she closed her eyes trying to pretend their world was right side up again. She kissed her husband on his forehead as she squeezed her muscles and pushed out his semi-hard love stick.

She wrapped herself in the sheet from the bed as she went to the bathroom to clean up and get dressed. Mandell followed her into the perfectly tiled bathroom and watched as Lena smiled and cleaned her body. She wanted to take a shower, but refused to undress completely and she had her reasons.

Her husband's inevitable question came as she was stepping into her heels.

"Lena, where is my daughter?" Mandell asked.

"You have to trust that she is somewhere safe." Clarke returned.

"Lena, my brother is dead and that was my best friend. Edwina is the best part of me."

Lena grimaced as Mandell continued.

"She didn't ask to come to this world. I sent for her, the day I had unprotected sex with her mother."

"Don't open this can of worms with me Mandell. We just had sex for the first time in months and you are talking about the day you had sex with that bitch."

"Don't call her a bitch Lena. She's really nice."

Before Mandell could speak again, Lena slapped him so hard his head turned and spit flew across the room.

"She slept with my husband. What should I call her, a nun and why do you care what I call her. If you'd been that concerned with me instead of laying up with the first whore you thought could take your pain away, we wouldn't be here. You should have waited to share the burdens of your life with me. I'm your wife. Why didn't you trust me with what you'd done? I know this life is hard, but I would have been there for you. The fucked up part is that you trusted a complete stranger with the most intimate part of you. Mandell, you shared your fears with someone else. That is what's so fucked up. Sex is sex, but she knows a part of you that you always hid from me and this is unacceptable." Lena explained as her hopes to save her marriage diminished by the second.

"Baby, I know you're upset, but let's not talk about Tesha right now. I just want to see my daughter. I have to know that she is okay."

"Well, Mandell. The young beauty is fine."

"Take me to my baby, Lena." Mandell said as his voice trembled. "Don't take her from me."

"And what about her mother? Is she going to let us take Edwina and raise her as our own?" Lena asked.

"Hell no." Mandell answered before realizing it.

"Well, then. They'll just have to hang tight until we can work something out." Lena answered.

"There is nothing to figure out or maybe there is. Contrary to what you may think, I would never hurt your daughter, but I'm not so sure about her mother. I have to know if she knew about me and and if she did I'm gonna fuck both of you up." Lena said as she channeled her Mafietta.

"You still ask questions as if you're Mandell The King, but I think you forget that you are Mandell The Bitch. My bitch, remember?"

Mandell fought the urge to snap Lena's neck. He was nobody's bitch and it was time she knew it. He just needed to know that his daughter was okay.

"Cut the fucking dramatics, Lena. Where are Tesha and Edwina?"

He waited for Lena to respond and when she didn't the anger spread through him and he wanted his next line to cut his child-less bride to her core.

"Where is my family Lena? You are so quick to kidnap people, but if you could have given me a child, this never would have happened."

Lena immediately doubled over as if someone had two pieced her in the gut. Mandell's words cut her like a knife all the way down to her broken spirit and empty womb. Tears fell from her face to the floor like waterfalls as Mandell used one of the two weapons he had left to force his wife into submission.

"Lena wiped her tears and stood up to face her husband. She walked within inches of his face and while he expected her to spit on him or slap him again. She reached out, caressed his face and said, "You have no idea how much I loved you."

She kissed him on the cheek and headed for the door. Mandell saw that his first tactic didn't work, so he employed the second one.

"Turn around Lena." He said with a shiny new gun pointing her in the face.

Suddenly her dream came flooding back to her. Again, her spirit whispered to the body that housed it. She would never have his undivided affection and now as she stared down the barrel of his gun she knew it.

"Try me." Lena said as she turned the knob.

Lena heard the shot before she felt its effects it seemed. Maybe her body was in shock, but she screamed as she fell to the floor. A piercing pain seemingly ripped through her shoulder. She reached to inspect the area as a pain induced smile covered her face.

She opened her eyes to see Mandell standing over her with the gun pointed at her face.

"Here's how this is gonna happen. You are gonna get up and tell those guys we're working things out and we're going to get Tesha and my baby."

"Fuck Tesha and your baby." Lena said as her hand slid underneath the arm of shirt and puller her small piece from its holder.

Mandell allowed Lena to stand. He watched her as she rubbed her hand up and down her arm. He no longer felt bad for firing off at her. This was his chance to have Julius give him whatever he wanted. There was no way he was letting her go. He walked over to his wife and placed the gun on her forehead.

"You have 5 seconds to tell me where my daughter is or I will blow your fucking brains out." Mandell growled.

There it was. Lena had her answer and there was no denying it now. She quickly pulled the small petite gun from the oversized arm of her shirt and wasted no time plugging three bullets into his chest.

She screamed as he fell to the floor and blood gushed all over the Bellow's new carpet. Jackal and Tiger rushed in to find Lena collapsed on the floor looking at her dying husband cough up blood.

Tiger grabbed Mandell's gun and laughed as he pulled out the clip and started to throw the rubber bullets at him.

"Did you think we'd give you real bullets, Nigga?" Jackal asked.

"Fuck you and fuck you too Lena." He whispered as the life seeped from him.

"Nah, Nigga – Fuck you." She said as she stood over the man she once loved and shot him once more in the dick.

She handed Jackal the gun and left the room.

Damn she thought as her hands shook. Her fucking dream had just come true.

17 THE ROAD FROM HERE

Clarke sat on the bed watching Lena pack. She'd spent the last 3 days with her new friend. Killing someone, even it was deemed self-defense, could be a heavy burden to bear. Clarke was happy to help Lena work through it all.

They'd even come up with a plan that would lead the entire family away from the darkness of drugs and murder. Their money, especially when combined, was enough to give wings to any business.

Lena exhaled as she zipped the last suitcase.

"Thanks for everything Clarke. I really don't know what I would have done without you."

"I only did what I hope you would have done for me if the roles were reversed." Clarke returned with a small smile.

Lena rushed over to hug the new woman she called her sister.

"Next time we meet, it's gonna be to write checks and get this thing started, right?"

"Yes, we have a meeting with the new project manager next week." Clarke answered.

"Can you believe we're finally moving on up?" Lena asked.

"Yep, I sure can." Clarke smiled as she thought of the bright future she and Lena created for The Port City Kings.

The men were assembled on the other end of the great mansion. Magnus, Julius, Akmed, Errol, and Admiral closed the business plan Lena and Clarke submitted.

"This will work, gentleman." Magnus' lawyer commented. "The idea is solid and it will bring you guys a shit load of greenbacks."

"That's what we like to hear." Akmed said, always ready to make another dollar.

"This is a proud day for The Port City Kings." Julius commented.

"I knew our girls were smart, but this takes the cake." Magnus returned.

Errol and Admiral sat back and nodded their heads in agreement. Clarke and Lena were taking The Kings to the next level in business and it felt good. Errol was proud of his wife and now they'd be out of the game in one year just as Magnus said.

The room was full of proud men that day. Men who plotted a promising future with their leading ladies at the helm.

Tesha and Edwina were escorted back to their home in The Keys. Their cabinets were stocked and Edwina's room remodeled. There was a small envelope on the kitchen counter. Tesha wiped her eyes as she opened the note.

Dear Edwina,

There is no way I'd ever leave you if I had a choice, sweet baby. There is so much I wanted to teach you. If money were time, you'd have no worries and while I won't be there in flesh – I will always be there for you in spirit. I have made every financial provision for you possible. That was the least I could do.
I love you baby girl,
Daddy

Tesha screamed as her suspicions were confirmed. Mandell was dead. There was one more card, one addressed to her. She opened it and while she expected a letter from her paramour, she found a pre-paid Visa card and a budget instead.

Damn, this gravy train has run out, she thought as she wiped the last tear from her eyes and looked over at HER daughter. She ripped Mandell's note to pieces as she reached for her phone.

"Edwina, let's call your Daddy." She said as she hit #1 on her speed dial.

"Somebody finally offed his ass." She smiled into the receiver. "Baby, now you can come home for good."

Then she smiled as she hung up and headed to her stocked pantry to make dinner for her REAL family.

ABOUT THE MAFIETTA NOVELLA SERIES

The Mafietta Novella Series takes the reader through Clarke's tough romantic past and the devastating things she deals with on her way to finding love. It explains how a woman, so tired of bullshit, can consciously fall in love with someone whose life is full of it.

Connect with Author E.W. Brooks via:

Facebook
https://www.facebook.com/EWBrooks

Twitter   @mafiettaishere

Instagram   ewbrooksbooks

Official Site   www.Mafietta.com

Made in the USA
Las Vegas, NV
20 January 2022